FALLOUT

NICK MANNS

Hodder
Children's
Books

A division of Hodder Headline Limited

CAMDEN LIBRARIES

Thank you:
**Beverley Birch, Amarjit Chana, Bev Francis,
Loralynn Gosling, Pat Kelly, Ranvir Singh, Phil Tear,
Lucy Courtenay, Neelam Khanna.**

And, as always, Bel, Ellie and Harvey

Copyright © 2004 Nick Manns

First published in Great Britain in 2004
by Hodder Children's Books

The right of Nick Manns to be identified as the Author
of the Work has been asserted by him in accordance with
the Copyright, Designs and Patents Act 1988.

2 4 6 8 10 9 7 5 3

A Catalogue record for this book is available from
the British Library

ISBN 0 340 85567 3

Typeset in Bembo by Avon Dataset Ltd,
Bidford-on-Avon, Warwickshire

Printed and bound in Great Britain by
Clays Ltd, St Ives plc

The paper and board used in this paperback by
Hodder Children's Books are natural recyclable products made from
wood grown in sustainable forests. The manufacturing processes
conform to the environmental regulations of the country of origin.

Hodder Children's Books
a division of Hodder Headline Limited
338 Euston Road
London NW1 3BH

FALLOUT

About the Author

in Kettering with my wife, two children and several
s.

Three days a week I catch a train into Leicester and
work with dyslexic students at Leicester College. On the
other days, I stay at home and try and work on my writing.
sometimes I am successful.

When I was a child, my father was in the RAF and we
travelled around a lot. I spent many years living in strange
houses with a growing collection of books and a map on
the wall, telling me where we'd ended up.

I've been living in my current, rickety house, for 14
years now, and I have no intention of moving again.
Sometimes, in the night, I hear the sound of footsteps on
the stairs, but I no longer worry about ghosts – it's usually
my daughter coming home anyway.

I mostly write in the mornings, in an attic room that
looks out on a busy main road. I sometimes spend the
afternoons cycling through the countryside. As with cycling,
I prefer to know where my stories are headed, so I often
make elaborate notes. I occasionally draw maps as well.

I think I'm pretty lucky to have the time to make up
people and places: I started doing it years ago, when I was
six or seven, and I haven't stopped since.

Nick Manns' debut novel *Control-Shift* was shortlisted for
the North East Book Award and the Branford Boase
Award, longlisted for the Carnegie Medal, and nominated
for the Stockton Award. *Dead Negative* has been shortlisted
for The South Lanarkshire Book Award.

For David
in memory of our shared lives

For David
In memory of our shared love

One

No one knew he was there.

There were a couple of students tapping away on the far side; a white woman with spiky hair writing on a spreadsheet. Some kind of supervisor, he thought. Hardly looked up when he came in, that first time. Late afternoon, on Monday. Three days ago.

'Help yourself,' was all she said and carried on with her figuring.

Greg walked behind her desk to a computer in a row of six. Tried to look like he knew the place; felt like a burglar when the owner arrives home. Dropped his folder on the table and eased himself into the seat.

There were tall windows behind; wooden floorboards below. The door was open so he had a good look out. No other exit, so that if it came to a jam, he was stuck like a moth spiked to a card.

He pulled Raff's red folder from the bag, and opened

the section marked 'Psychology'. A page scribbled in Raff's blue scrawl.

There was a stink of old polish and he could hear the murmur of voices down the corridor. He rubbed his eyes and poked the power button with his forefinger. Listened to the fan turning over and waited while the screen did its binary stuff.

'Take a few seconds,' Raff said, and Greg had just shrugged.

When the ID box appeared, he tapped in 'mgraves'. Like Raff said, 'Michael Graves – my name.'

Greg leaned back and looked at the ceiling; at the light cables stretching up three metres; at the dust floured across the shades. Remembered that Raff had told him the college would be empty. 'Study week,' he said. 'No students around. I'm still registered there – you'll be OK.'

'Password?' the screen said and he tapped out 'headman', his fingers flashing the keys, the letters turned into stars. Hit return.

The screen dissolved and the greeting: 'Welcome, Michael Graves' appeared.

He was in.

He pushed Raff's spare disk into the slot; opened a new file. Wondered where to begin, how to set off. Seven days on Raff's floor and he was still circling the starting place. Didn't even know who to write to. A quick email and the college would be swarming with police. He knew that now.

That first night, when he'd arrived, he simply told Raff everything. Sitting in the lounge with the bag at his feet, heavy with its dirty secret.

'Stuff's dangerous,' Raff said, glancing down. 'You know that. You have to keep it safe, away from people.'

'Yeah,' Greg said. 'I know of a place. Down by the canal.'

And they'd looked at each other in the low light; a plane tree shivering outside and the touch of death resting at their feet.

'Nuff to make you paranoid,' Raff said. 'Watch your back everyways.'

Yeah, right, he'd thought. Nuff to make you leap at your own face in a glass.

He turned back to the screen. Touched the keys. Made a start.

Two

I haven't killed anyone. Let's get that straight. After all the lies that Bonnington has told, I am innocent. As for the rest – plenty of people are dead – and I now know why.

To begin with? – I'd been sick for a fortnight – off school and really out of it. When I got to Garfield that Monday, Suli had crossed the form room and said something like: 'We've been split for Maths.'

Straight out. Like it was stuff he'd been bottling up. I didn't follow what he was on about, not straight away. There was the usual din going on and Mr Everett was trying to sort out work experience forms. Suli said that he was working with this head-case, Deadman. Had to have a new partner because of some stupid project.

'Oh,' I said, trying to act cool. 'Really?'

Maths was second lesson, straight after English with Mrs Mitchell. He met Dilshad outside the library

4

and they made their way up the two flights.

The others were scattered outside room 32 and Sandeep Singh shouted: 'Hello, skiver!' when he saw Greg.

'You're nowhere, man,' Greg said. 'Get lost.' Took a look in the window opposite; hair greased; tie like a string of liquorice; white shirt draining colour from his face.

'Nice to see you, Greg,' said Suzie Marlowe, tipping a smile as she waltzed past. 'Been a long time –'

'Since when?' he said.

'Since she saw your cheesy face,' said Suli, giving him a push.

When Jordan appeared, a couple of minutes later, he was with Mrs Yardley, the Year Head, and a large Asian girl. They stood at the far end of the corridor, and he heard Jordan say, 'Don't worry, we'll get it sorted.' Then Yardley went back to her office and Jordan and the girl came down to the classroom.

She stood back as Jordan bent to open the door, eyes downcast. Waited whilst Jordan shouted: 'Hold it – you, David Wheatley – back of the queue –'

Yeah, Greg thought. Heil Hitler to you too.

Then they were in, Greg following the others; winking at Suzie Marlowe as she took her place on the far side. He went over and dropped his gum in the bin, stood by Jordan's desk, hands stuffed in his pockets, bag at his feet.

'OK, settle down,' said Jordan, standing in front of the chalkboard. 'Coats off, bags on the floor,' and he turned to the Asian girl. 'It's Inderjit? Is that right? Inderjit Sandhu?'

'Yes,' she said quietly.

'Right,' he said, to the rest of the class. 'You know what you have to do – so get on with it.'

'Hello?' said Greg. 'Only take a sec, Mr Jordan. But where shall I plant my sad ass?'

Jordan looked up at him, eyes narrowing, as if deciding whether or not to take the bait.

'Ah, Greg,' he said. 'Feeling better?' and without waiting for a reply, he turned to Inderjit and said, 'Greg Price. He's just come back from illness. Shingles wasn't it?'

'Yeah,' he said. 'Something like that.'

'Well –?' said Jordan. 'Take a seat while I get Inderjit sorted out.'

Greg pushed his fingers through his hair; took a slow-motion bow and collected his bag; wandered to the space in front of Sheetal and Davindar.

'Hi, girls,' he said. 'Nice to see you again.'

'Yeah,' said Sheetal, pulling gum from her mouth. 'What you have anyway?'

'Shingles,' he said, and leaned back against the wall; grinned at Suzie.

'Sounds like something you get off a beach —' said Davindar. 'Geddit — Greg?' nudging Sheetal. 'Off a beach!'

Jordan looked across, eyebrows raised. 'Pipe down,' he said. 'While I get everything sorted. You — Davindar — I don't want to hear from you again. This lesson.'

'Charming!' she said. 'Blame me, why don't you?' Tossing hair away from her face.

But he had his hearing appliance turned off, or else didn't care to tango. Stood up and said: 'OK, we're into the second week. Of the project. Everyone — all pairs — should have handed in their topics. Last Wednesday.'

'What if we want to change our idea?' said Akhil, at the front. 'Do something different?'

'Like — something more interesting,' said Philip Wiseman at the back. He was sitting so far down that his armpits were level with the desk top.

'Thank you, Philip,' said Mr Jordan, eyebrows raised again. Trying to keep it light.

'Thang queue, Philip,' echoed Carl Fraser. 'Thang queue.' His mouth stretching the sounds, making them foreign. Eyes like stone.

'Carl?' said Jordan. 'Do you want to stay in the class

or would you like to discuss your progress with Mrs Yardley?'

Fraser looked down, grinning. 'You're OK, sir,' he said. 'I'm just ready to rock and roll.'

'Good,' said Jordan. Greg touched his temple at Fraser in mock salute; smiled at Suzie, who stuck her tongue out.

'OK,' said Jordan, looking round the room. 'If you want to change your idea, let me have it by – the end of today's lesson. Yeah?'

Sheetal tapped Greg on the back. 'Thing is,' she said, 'who's Jordan going to place you with? I mean, you've got to be in a pair – and everyone is already spoken for – except –' and she fluttered her eyelashes at the new student. 'Could be your lucky day, Gregory: your chance for a hot date!' And both girls had shrieked so loudly that Jordan had looked up and said: 'Be quiet! The pair of you!'

He allowed the sudden silence to lengthen; watched until everyone was looking down at their books, avoiding his stare, then he turned back to Inderjit.

'The class is working in pairs. On different surveys: finding out which students have packed lunches, for example – or those who come to school by bus. Then the information has to be presented mathematically, using histograms and pie charts and so on.'

Greg stuck his hand up in a slow-mo fascist salute. He said: 'Mr Jordan – any danger of getting something to do? Today?' Hitting the second syllable; changing the tone. Suzie Marlowe looked up, grinning.

'We don't do sarcasm in this class,' said Jordan. 'No future in it.'

He shrugged. 'Not what I've heard.'

Jordan said, 'As soon as I've finished with Inderjit, you can get started.' And then, as an afterthought: 'You'll be working together.'

Greg snorted, looked down. Ignored the sniggers from behind. Sheetal saying: 'Told you so.' Even Suzie Marlowe found the idea entertaining. Hilarious.

Two minutes later and Jordan was leading the new student across. Motioned her to the seat next to Greg's. Said: 'This is Inderjit Sandhu.'

He nodded: 'I heard.'

'You've picked up the idea of the project? From the discussion?' said Jordan.

'Yeah,' he said, and lifted his pencil, drew a box on his Maths book.

'Good. There's a help sheet,' Jordan said. 'With examples.'

'Right –'

'So, I'll leave you two. To get acquainted,' said Jordan, walking away, ignoring the laughter from the back row; from Sheetal and Davindar.

'You're funny,' Greg said. 'Think I've split my shirt.'

Three

Inderjit placed a Leicester City FC pencil case on the table and pushed the 'help' sheet between them. He looked across, casually; saw the page was divided into paragraphs of explanation, examples of how to illustrate evidence.

'Looks tricky,' he said and drew some more boxes. 'A real "brain" teaser.'

'Sorry?' she said, looking at the side of his face. 'I don't follow.'

He stopped drawing, looked up. 'That –' pointing at the sheet. 'It's just – tedious –' and he yawned loudly to make the point.

'Depends,' she said.

'Oh, yeah,' he said. 'Of course – I didn't know that.'

'Depends if you've got the imagination,' she said, flipping the sheet over, 'or not.'

'Ooh,' said Sheetal behind. 'A lover's tiff.'

'Get lost, Sheet-al,' he said.

'Doesn't have to be something "sad",' Inderjit said.

'We're talking Maths?' he said. 'In school? This isn't sitting on a theme park high ride. Waiting for the corkscrew.' He leaned back, grinning.

She put down her pencil; looked at his face as if studying a particular problem. She said: 'I don't know what your difficulty is – whether it's because I'm fat and black or whether you've got an ego the size of three counties. But you better decide whether or not you want to do something with what we've got here.'

He just grunted – shrugged his shoulders – and Jordan had said something crass about it being the first time he'd heard Greg Price lost for words.

'Not lost,' he replied. 'Just too polite. Is all.'

But it was too late by then. All he could hear was the mocking tinkle of Inderjit's bangles, the jeer from Wiseman and Fraser; Sheetal sniggering.

It didn't help, Jordan telling everyone to settle down; Inderjit suggesting that they brainstorm a few ideas.

He took his time packing his bag when the bell had finished; turned a cold face to Suzie Marlowe when she'd said: 'See you later, three counties,' as she trudged out past him.

'Got a mouth on her,' Suli had said, as they'd

mooched towards the canteen. 'Mouth and a half, that Inderjit'.

'Yeah,' he said, hands stuffed deep in his pockets; a scowl taped to his face.

His mother was listening to a radio play when he pushed back the front door, dropped his bag at the foot of the stairs.

'Is that you, Greg?' she called from the lounge, as he headed for the kitchen.

'Nope – Ghost of Christmas Past,' he said, running the cold tap and filling a glass.

'How'd you get on?' she said, coming into the kitchen, mug in one hand and newspaper in the other. Skin the colour of puke.

He put the glass down. 'So-so,' he said. 'Got some dope to share with in Maths. Girl from Leicester.'

'Yes?' his mother said, as if she imagined the conversation was the Orient Express and about to depart.

'Well – that's it. Nothing else,' he said.

'You feel – all right – and everything?'

'Yeah,' he said, brushing past her. 'Terrific.' And over his shoulder: 'What's for tea?'

Hearing her mutter something about lasagne as he hauled his bag up the stairs.

At the top, I came face to face with the photograph of Sarah, my sister. Four years younger and dead when I was seven. The picture captures her blue-eyed curiosity – as if she was trying to make sense of the dark hole of Dad's camera.

I saw her every time I went up the stairs – and I thought about her each and every day. My mother said that she refused to allow Sarah to simply fade away: like we needed to remember that she'd once been with us.

But the picture was as heavy as a boulder – and my mother was too slow to understand that.

Four

Twenty-four hours later he was standing outside the Year Head's office with Carl Fraser. It was 3.30 and above the drone of a polisher, he could hear voices from inside Mrs Yardley's room.

Fraser was staring away to his left, towards the Special Needs area. He leaned against the wall, bag at his feet, hands in his pockets. If Fraser had the nerve and turned his way, Greg would see the red stain on Fraser's cheek; the bruise that would slowly turn dark. It was going to hang around for the next week, like a daily reminder of the fist Greg had planted in Fraser's face.

Greg shifted his feet, recalled the moment, when they were on the ground, punching and kicking – snarling at one another; the other kids gathering round, chanting 'fight, fight.'

It had ended with the voice of the geography teacher, Mr Stevens, pushing his way through the crowd, and pulling them apart. 'All right, all right,' he'd said, hauling them to their feet. Greg leaning into Fraser's face, snarling: 'Say that again – and I'll kill you.'

When the door opened, Mr Stevens emerged and then Mrs Yardley was at the entrance saying: 'OK, Greg: come inside.'

A couple of filing cabinets, a plant on the window shelf; family photos and a large desk that straddled the narrow room. Hadn't changed in three years, he thought, pulling the chair back from her desk.

'You want me to siddown?' he said.

'Yes,' she said, looking like she'd lost a winning lottery ticket. Allowed the seconds to tick by on her wall clock. Then the quiet voice, the direct stare: 'So, tell me: what happened?'

He looked down at his feet. Said: 'Fraser came out. Made some cheap remark. I hit him.' He spread his palms: 'That's it.'

'What did he say?'

'It doesn't matter. You wouldn't understand, anyway.' He looked at her and smiled. 'Mrs Yardley – I know I shouldn't have whacked Fraser. Sorry – tell me what the punishment is – then we can all go home.'

She smiled for a moment, allowed her finger-tips to touch the folder on her desk.

'That's very thoughtful,' she said, 'considerate. But I'd

really like to get to the bottom of this.' She paused: 'Why were you so wound up?'

She had the kind of neat, made-up face that you expect to see on TV – reading the news – or fronting a programme on holiday destinations. Short fair hair, with maybe a hint of red. Touch of lipstick. As efficient as bleach.

She said: 'You've just come back to school. You were sick?'

'Yeah,' he said. 'I caught shingles. Had a couple of weeks off.'

'And you're better?'

She was trying to win his confidence, he could see that.

'Yeah – I'm OK now.' And he smiled back.

'So, what did Carl Fraser say, that got under your skin?'

He leaned back, thought about it. Pieced together the events of the day while staring out through the window behind Mrs Yardley.

That morning, Suli had offered him a lemon drop when Greg had sauntered on to the playground at the back of the school.

'Here,' Suli said, offering him the bag.

'Nar, you're all right,' Greg replied and took a seat on the bench next to Dilshad. Watched the other kids kicking a ball around, whilst Suli told them both the plot of this SF film he'd caught on satellite that last night.

He was looking over Suli's head towards the spinney on the sports field, when he heard footsteps behind; was aware of the change of light, and the next moment he felt a jab in the side and Suli was burbling: 'Someone for you, mate,' his face tipped into a top-to-bottom smile.

And Greg knew, even before he looked up, who it was; who would be waiting there. Inderjit Sandhu. In all her largeness. Clear brown eyes and hair parted down the middle; school bag by her side. She said: 'Greg?'

He didn't answer for a second; gave himself time to reflect. 'Yeah?' he said.

'About Maths? I have an idea. About the project –' and she'd looked across at Suli and Dilshad, both trying not to laugh.

'Oh, really?' he said, aware of the scuffle of feet ahead; the soft thump of the football. 'Sounds really interesting.' Hearing the splutter of the other two.

She frowned, paused as if making up her mind, and then pulled her bag over her shoulder, '– but I'll tell you later. At a better time,' and she turned and headed off towards the library.

'That's quite some girl,' Dilshad said.

'Yeah,' said Suli. 'Big enough for you, Greg?'

And he grunted. Got up and said: 'See you,' and headed for the Humanities entrance. The voice of Suliman calling after him: 'She's not that bad!' with Dilshad adding, 'Yeah, but she is that big!'

'Was it something that Carl said?'

Mrs Yardley was looking at him curiously, her head tilted to one side.

Yeah, that's right Mrs Y, he thought. You win tonight's star prize. It was something that Fraser had said.

After English, at the end of the morning, not due to go into dinner until 12.30, Suli had gone to play in a five-a-side tournament, Greg wandered down the stairs and out through the fire doors. He hadn't stepped more than a couple of metres when he felt a tap on his arm.

Inderjit said: 'Have you got a minute?' Raising her carefully shaped eyebrows.

'Yeah,' he said, looking about him. 'Why not?'

So they walked over to the bench, and she'd said, 'Why don't we do some research. On sickness. In the county?'

'Eh?' he said, trying to grasp what she was on about.

'Oh, I don't know. Something like lung cancer or heart disease—'

'What do you mean?' still not getting it.

'Well,' she said, sitting down on the bench and looking up at him, 'we could get some information off the internet. From the Health Authority. And we could look at which illnesses are – you know – common – in the county—'

'You take all this crap seriously, don't you?' he said, allowing a smile to ease itself on to his face. 'Like this stuff is important. It's only Maths. And we're talking Jordan here.' He looked back towards the library, checked there was no one he knew lurking around, waiting to give him a hard time.

'Oh, don't give me that – that – tough guy stuff.' She stood up, looked him in the face, said: 'My grandfather is dying of leukaemia. In Hindlip. I want to find out – more. And the worst thing is, I've got this chance – and I'm stuck with this child who's pretending to be grown up and mature—'

'Oh,' he said, looking up, 'anyone I know?'

'Hi, Greg,' called Carl Fraser, strolling over with Philip Wiseman. 'How're you doing? Oh – I see you've got company,' smirking as he looked at Inderjit.

'It's OK. I'll see you later,' she said, picking up her bag and moving away.

'Got yourself fixed up there,' said Fraser, watching her walk off. 'Nice girl, eh?' pushing his arm. 'Sorting out a date – eh?'

'Watch your mouth, Fraser,' he'd said, standing up.

'Girls have to watch out when he's about,' Wiseman had added, nodding.

Greg said nothing, dropped his bag. Waited.

'Bet you think you're a bit of a lady killer – eh?' said Fraser, and shoved his arm again. A broad grin pushing across his narrow face; amusement in his cold eyes. 'Should be a warning when you're around: girls beware. Eh, Greg?'

Greg shook off Fraser's hand, felt the heat rise into his face; heard Fraser say: 'Haven't trodden on your feelings, have I, killer?' And that's when he hit him. When he pulled back his fist and jabbed it into Fraser's face. Feeling the pain across his knuckles; seeing Fraser stumble, hand to his cheek. Wiseman yelling out.

'So,' said Mrs Yardley, 'what did he say?'

Five

'What happened?'

His father at the end of the dining table. Greg's yellow report card next to his plate. A letter from Mrs Yardley smoothed out in front.

'A misunderstanding,' he said. 'This boy—'

'Excuse m-me, Greg,' said his father, looking at him through his thick lenses, left hand touching the card. 'This isn't the result of a m-m-misunderstanding.'

The lenses magnified his eyes, the lines at the corners. Made his whole face look as if he was staring at him. A face of large grey eyes. Fixed, unblinking. And the stammer? Always got worse when he was anxious. Or angry. Like however hard he tried to cover his feelings, they blurted out of his mouth like a learner driver with a bad case of the shakes.

'Don't know how to put it, then.'

His father sighed and looked down; his mouth like a crease in a sheet. 'You've never – been in any trouble –

22

nothing serious – before. What was it that – made – you – react – with v-v-violence?' One hand clasped over the other. The direct stare.

'Don't remember,' he said, listening to the sound of his mother in the kitchen, moving trays out of the oven. 'Fraser's a git: he irritated me. It was a wind-up or something. I felt – tired –'

His father said: 'In her letter, Mrs Yardley said that you weren't able to explain to her – what led to this – incident. You have to share with – Inderjit, is it – in Maths?'

'Yes – Look,' and he glanced at his father. 'I got irritated with Fraser because – he was being a klutz. You understand that, don't you? – About my having to work with a girl?'

'Yes?'

'Well, that's it. I – hit him,' and he shrugged, head bent.

He could hear the sound of his mother lifting plates; the slip-slop of her feet coming down the corridor.

'Sorry it's taken so long,' she said, face flushed with heat from the kitchen. 'Got the timing for the baked potatoes slightly out.'

And when the three of them were sat down, his father said: 'Christine, I've discussed the report c-c-card.'

'Yes?' said his mother, her face lifted in enquiry. Like he was telling her about some business meeting he'd had that day; explaining that the clutch was slipping on the car.

'Yes,' his father said, lifting his fork. 'Greg had a "misunderstanding" with this other boy.' He looked down at the letter Mrs Yardley had written. 'A Carl Fraser.' He paused, and then drew a line through his meat. 'Do we know this – ah – Carl Fraser?'

'No, Dad,' he'd said, interrupting. 'You've never met him. Just some kid. Lives up on Albion.'

'I see,' said his father, looking at him. 'But that doesn't give you the – the r-r-right to go around h-h-hitting people –'

'– never said it did,' he said, feeling his face heat up, his heart begin to bang.

His father looked across at him. He said: 'You're big enough, Greg, to keep c-c-control of your temper. You're not a s-s-seven-year-old now.'

A cheap hit, Dad, he thought. That's below the belt, even from a low-life like you. But he said nothing, suddenly empty of words; his dead sister's face filling the room.

After tea, after I'd cleared the stuff and washed the plates and cutlery, I went into the lounge and told my mother I was going for a swim. She just looked up from her book and said OK. Gave her Mona Lisa smile.

I didn't bother telling Dad what I was doing, because that would have invited more pointless chat; a further lecture about 'im-m-m-m-maturity' and 'r-r-responsibilities' – that kind of thing. I simply pushed my bike down the hall and headed across town.

There was a scattering of people in the pool and he took one of the far lanes; worked his way back and forth for the next hour; tumble turns at each end and lengths every forty seconds. Allowed his head to fill with the quiet voice of Mrs Yardley.

It was after she had explained the details of the report card, and before she closed the file, that she had looked across her desk and said: 'How are you getting on with Inderjit?'

Clean off the script; totally left field.

'What do you mean?' he said. 'She sits next to me in Maths.' What else was there to say?

Mrs Yardley closed the folder and rested her hands lightly on its cover. 'I don't want this to go any further, Greg, but – Inderjit could do with a decent break.' Face unsmiling, serious. 'Her life has been quite – difficult recently, and we were hoping that you might be a sympathetic partner.'

He said nothing. Waited for the explanation.

'You don't have to do anything,' Mrs Yardley said. 'Just be friendly.' She smiled: 'That OK?'

'Yeah, fine,' he said. There was no explanation; no further details. He reached over and took the report card. Left the room with a headful of questions.

An hour in the water and he touched the side at the end of seventy lengths. Held on to the edge and wiped his face. The pool had filled up since his arrival. There were kids splashing in the shallow end; groups of adults hanging out. He ducked under the lane dividers and waded towards the far side, thinking of school.

He hadn't got as far as the steps in the corner when he felt a hand touch his arm, heard a familiar voice say: 'Hi, killer – going to ignore me?' And looking down, he found himself staring into the face of Suzie Marlowe.

Six

'Didn't see you,' he said, and sank back.

Her hair hung loose and she wore a swimming costume that shimmered with orange and gold, like flames beneath the surface. Head and shoulders out of the water; dark blue eyes and a smile that touched her lips like a passing butterfly. A trace of perfume above the swimming-pool stink.

He didn't know what to say. Was aware of the echo; the schoolkids all around.

'You were really – into it – over there,' she said, smiling.

'Yeah. Come here every week. Do a few lengths –'

'So, what happened – with Fraser – today? No one's saying.'

He shrugged. Looked at where Lorraine Gillespie was approaching from the deep end, fair hair tied back, face glistening.

'Just a disagreement,' he said. 'Got a bit –'

'– out of hand?'

'Yeah.'

Suzie looked amused. Bobbed hair curving beneath her chin; smile that pulled dimples into her cheeks. 'Darren Bridges said you hit Fraser.'

There was a sudden splash and Lorraine planted her feet on the floor and rubbed water away from her face. 'Hi, Greg!' she said. 'Saw you over in the lanes. Thought of giving you a race but Suzie said you'd already taken a beating today.' Flicking water in his direction.

'Was saying – to Greg – that no one's talking. 'Bout that thing. With Fraser.'

Lorraine leaned back. 'That so?' she said.

''s nothing,' he said, shrugging. Looked up at the wooden boards of the roof.

'Well, go on,' said Suzie, 'you'll have to – you know – tell us what it's about.'

He looked down, looked from one face to the other. 'It's just stupid stuff,' rubbing his nose between thumb and forefinger.

They let the silence lap around them; the two girls staring at his face until Lorraine said: 'Fair enough,' and started back towards the deep end; wet hair trailing at the back of her neck.

'There's a party – next week – at Catherine's house

– Glenbrook Drive? You going?' asked Suzie; light pressure on the pronoun. Gentle curiosity.

'Hadn't – heard about it –'

'Do now,' she said. 'I'm going. Got the invite.'

She sank lower; allowed water to fill her mouth, let it fountain out.

'Yeah?' he said. 'So you could ask me?'

Out of the corner of his eye he could see that Lorraine had already made the turn, was already pulling her way down the pool. Twenty seconds away, less.

'Are you asking me out – on a date – Gregory Price?' said Suzie, pulling back, eyes wide. 'Asking me to go with you to the party?'

'Why not?' he said. 'Unless you've got yourself sorted.'

He could hear Lorraine's breathing by now; the splash of water.

'I'll let you know then, Gregory,' Suzie said and turned to face her friend. 'Gregory hasn't heard – about Catherine Baker's do – on the 5th. Thinks he might like to go. If he can find a date. For the evening.'

'That so?' said Lorraine. 'You're looking for a female to go with? Heard that Inderjit Sandhu was a bit of "all right",' – both girls turning and grinning at him.

'You want to ask her, Gregory,' Suzie said. 'She's a real "knock out", or so I've heard.'

Back at the house, up in his room, James Dean wasn't talking.

Staring from the poster tacked to his door: white shirt, tie like a noose and eyes that said 'Yeah?' But he had nothing to say.

Cleaned out, eh James? Greg thought. Know the feeling.

He dropped a CD on to the player and lay back on his bed. Let thoughts of Suzie Marlowe mingle with the shifts and turns of Dutch Elektro. What was that all about, he thought. Catherine Baker's party at the end of half-term: was that a come-on – or not?

He listened to the bass driving behind the synthesiser; the bhangra beat. Thought of Inderjit Sandhu and Yardley's request that he 'behave'; because Inderjit 'needed a break'. 'Tell me about it,' he said aloud and got up to change the disc, reaching for his dictionary on the way back.

He thumbed through the 'L's and looked for 'lewkemia', but there was nothing. The only word starting with 'lew' was 'lewd' and that meant 'exciting lust'.

I don't think so, he thought to himself. Not this time. He switched on the computer and checked the thesaurus.

'Leukaemia,' he read. 'A disease caused by the

overproduction of white blood cells.'

Four syllables that could easily have meant something else. Like an island in Greece. Mrs Hastings' daughter had died of leukaemia, he remembered. Their old next-door neighbour. Before he'd really got to know them.

He pointed the cursor at the internet icon, pulled down the FlameFirst search engine and ran a check. Downloaded fifteen pages from a helpline. Sat back and read the facts, his eyes flicking over the grey technical detail. Every so often talking to the silent shadow staring from the door.

'How does this sound, James?' he said, when he felt that he'd got some kind of grip on what he was reading. 'The white blood cells – that fight infection? Go into some kind of production frenzy and the result is that the marrow – the gunk in the middle of bones – is stuffed to bursting with these immature cells and they're of no use to man nor beast.' He looked up: 'That's leukaemia, James. Not a holiday resort in the Aegean, after all. Just a regular death sentence.'

Seven

He remembered that moment, those days later; leaning back in the college computer room and thinking of his old life. Of Suli and Dilshad; Suzie Marlowe's smile and Fraser's rat-like grin. Everything had seemed so screwed up back then – but what did he know.

A tall guy wearing a grey suit and rimless glasses came in to chat to the spreadsheet woman, bending low and muttering down at her. She said: 'How many?' And the tall guy cranked himself to his full height, and looked round the room, eyes flicking over the consoles and his lips moving. Counting the work stations, making a calculation.

He didn't see Inderjit until break the next day. He'd gone to the library to drop off *Strange Cosmos* and he saw her on the far side, working on one of the internet computers, a file of notes spread out and Sheetal and Davindar sharing the next machine.

He waited in the queue by the checkout and out of the corner of his eye, saw Davindar lean across to Inderjit; heard her say: 'Oh, look, Indie, there's your boyfriend.' Sheetal's hand in front of her mouth. 'He's a real hunk,' went on Davindar. 'Don't you think, Sheetal? We all fancy him, you know.' Rolling 'all' round her mouth like a marble.

He strolled to where they sat, looked at Inderjit who was scrolling through some article she'd downloaded; smiled at the two girls looking up at him; waited for the main chance.

'Looked up leukaemia. On the net,' he said, feeling ridiculous.

Her eyes flickered away from the screen. 'Yes?'

'Yeah,' he said. 'Something about it being a disease – of the blood. Too many white blood cells.' He reached into his bag for his notebook.

'We're impressed,' said Sheetal, eyes wide. 'So much effort for a first date.'

'Come on, Sheetal,' said Davindar, pointing through the library window. 'There's Ranvir.'

'See you, girls,' he said, as they got up. 'Try not to trip over your tongues.'

Davindar turned and gave him the finger as she walked out.

'So,' said Inderjit. 'Why the sudden interest?'

He shrugged. 'Haven't been called three counties in a while,' he said. 'Look –' glancing around. 'I may have been a bit of a plank – when you tried to – explain –'

'Yeah –'

'But, we had this neighbour – her daughter – about five, I think, well, she died of leukaemia. Don't remember her too clearly. But they went away –'

'Are you on a mission?' she said. 'Someone send you to "say sorry"?'

What do you want me to do, beg? he thought. He dropped his bag, took a seat. 'I looked up the stuff,' he said, and shrugged.

He was aware of the librarian staring at them; the shouts from the kids outside. Inderjit looking down at her notes. Thank you, Mrs Yardley, he thought. What a good idea to be friendly.

'We live out in Hindlip – village towards Harborough?' Inderjit said.

He nodded. Swallowed a yawn.

'Feels like I've left my life behind. In Leicester, I mean. Used to like walking down by the canal, feed the ducks.' She looked up at him, quickly. 'When I was a kid, there was this place we used to go – me and my mates. Canal on Western Boulevard – Mum never knew – she'd have had seven fits. There's a bridge that's painted black and white. We went underneath and climbed as far as this cross-piece.' She smiled. 'Used to leave each other messages, hidden behind the girder. Special meeting place.' She looked away, across the playground to the houses beyond. 'But that's all over. Dad's back in India. On business.'

She looked down and he could see that her bottom lip was trembling. Heard the voice of Mrs Yardley. 'You came to stay with your grandparents?' he said.

'That's it. That's right,' she said. 'Except – you know – my grandfather – he's dying of –' she gestured to her pile of notes, the stack of printouts – 'this stinking illness.'

The librarian was moving round now, picking up discarded books from the tables. She checked her watch, shouted, 'The library is closing in two minutes.'

'The thing is – he's the third person in the village to have leukaemia – in the last two years –'

'Right,' he said, brows drawn together – 'I don't know . . .' Again, that empty gesture.

'No, listen, that's way – way above the average. Not three hundred people in the village. It's more than – oh – loads of times the average. For the rest of the population.'

'Yeah – but – what are you getting at?' he said. 'Where's this all heading?'

'There's something out there – that's making these people sick. I need to find out what it is. That's all.'

Eight

'Something out there.'

Like the words spoken from a character in an SF film. Imagining the scene on the flight deck of some galaxy cruiser: 'There's something out there, captain. We don't know what it is, but we'll need to investigate.'

He could imagine Suli running with the phrase, turning it around every chance he got; the voice pumped up, American. Staring at a beaker in science, he'd say: 'There's something in there, Mrs Brown, and we need to investigate.' Parting a plate of chilli in the canteen, like a surgeon performing heart bypass: 'Something lumpy in here,' he'd say, holding up a chunk of meat, 'better investigate, Captain.'

A gag they'd run for months, years.

Greg forgot about Inderjit in the drudgery of RS before lunch and through the first half of French in the afternoon. Woke up when Mrs Sharp said: '*C'est important de decouvrir.*'

It is important to find out. *C'est important de savoir.* It is important to know.

Yeah? He thought, and drew a circle on his page. 'That's as maybe.'

In Maths, last thing, Inderjit said: 'Here's the stuff – what I've found.' She passed over a pile of sheets. Like they were old work mates. Suli over the aisle, raising an eyebrow.

'Incidence of leukaemia in the Oxfordshire Health Region, 1961–91,' he read, and flicked through the paragraphs. The printer had clipped the right-hand pages, so that the neat margin of words were turned into unfinished fragments. He rubbed his eyes, adjusted his shoulders.

Inderjit leaned across, flipped to page four. She said: 'See, everything is broken down, according to – ah – year, sex, age and – em – abode.'

'Right,' he said, and again, 'Right,' lifting the sheet and scanning the figures.

She watched as he checked the lines.

'They're – ah – it's hard to – you know – make sense of this,' he said, turning the page.

'It says here –' grabbing the sheets – 'there,' pointing

to a line half way down, 'that – well, there's a summary of the rise of leukaemia over the period. And there was an increase in the disease of .2 per cent. There –' her finger touching the place.

'Couldn't that – something like that just be – you know – some problem with the way the information was collected?' He leaned back, turned the corner of a page with his thumb. 'It's pretty – you know – small?' A quick, sideways glance.

She didn't say anything; chewed her bottom lip and for a moment, he thought she was going to cry. He said: 'Perhaps – maybe – if we studied this stuff some more – we could find out, you know – if there's anything significant – in the rise of sickness.'

'Yeah,' she said, 'if you like.' Sulky, angry, looking down into her bag and pulling out a tissue, so that she could blow her nose, get herself together. The kind of detail that wasn't lost on the glitter sisters. Sheetal leaned forward, said: 'Now look what you've done, Gregory. Belting Fraser one day and upsetting Indie the next.'

'Go suck a lemon,' he snapped, shifting in his seat.

The bus dropped him off by the London Road pool that night and he took the museum path down to the high street. Heard the crisp echo of his heels snapping on the pavement; hands stuffed deep in his pockets. Stopped to look at the display in the bookshop.

He saw the darkness of his face in the glass, thought about the way the day had collapsed into a heap, at the end of Maths. Just before he'd joined Fraser outside Mrs Yardley's room for the daily report card review.

He'd gone to his locker in the English area; had just pulled back the door to offload his stuff, when he heard a familiar voice.

'Heard you were getting on like a forest fire. With Inderjit Sandhu.'

Suzie Marlowe, with Lorraine Gillespie, pausing on their way out.

He shrugged. 'Just someone I work with,' he said, half-turning. 'No big deal –'

'Oh, really?' said Suzie, eyebrows raised. 'That's not what I heard.'

'What do you mean? I don't get it.'

The pair exchanged glances, faces pulled into laughter, sniggering even as Suzie said: 'And – is Inderjit – getting it?' – collapsing into one another, their voices burying the whine of the floor polisher further down the corridor. A real laugh and a half.

He reached into his bag and pulled out his maths book, placed it inside his locker; pushed the door to.

Turned the key. 'Careful, girls,' he said, slinging his bag over his shoulder, 'or you'll rupture something.'

'Sorry, Greg,' said Suzie, wiping her eyes, 'only – joking – so – there's nothing in the rumour, then – about you and –?'

'She's just another sad act I work with,' he said, 'that's it. See you later,' and made to walk back down the corridor, to the office by the hall. But of course he couldn't do that, because the way was blocked by another student.

Inderjit Sandhu was standing with her bag at her feet and her maths file in her hand. She looked at him closely, puzzled; trying to make sense of what she'd heard.

Then she hoisted her bag over her shoulder, turned on her heel and headed for the exit. He watched her walk away, her sharp, brisk stride tack-tacking over the polished floor.

There was a sudden outbreath next to him; the pressure of fingers against his arm: 'Got a bit of making up to do there, Greg,' whispered Suzie. 'No one likes to be called a sad act.'

Nine

James Dean still wasn't speaking when Greg dumped his stuff on the bed. Twenty to five on a Thursday afternoon and Dean just stood in the soft light, right hand clutching the top of the door; hair swept back and a smile that didn't add up to the time of day.

Greg stretched himself out; looked at the cobweb drifting from his light shade, allowed all the tension to ooze away. He could hear his mother moving around the kitchen; the soft bang of cupboard doors, the ring of cutlery being dropped on to the kitchen table.

The next moment, Suzie Marlowe's face came into view. They were standing in the ticket hall of the railway station; people queuing at the yellow windows; groups staring up at the departures board. She was wearing faded jeans and a T-shirt that said *Stairway to Heaven* in large, black type. A full-on smile: cheeks pressed into dimples.

She leaned into him, so that he could feel her breath on his face. She said: 'It's important not to trip over yourself, Greg,' and the next thing, he felt the warm rush of water closing over his head and he was sinking down into a black tunnel, mouth and nose stopped; the sharp taste of chlorine like a headful of bleach.

His hands reached up into the velvety darkness, trying to get a grip on something, trying to find some way to haul himself up, to grab a mouthful of air, but he just sank back, the darkness filling his lungs; his cry lost in the folds of the deep.

'Greg? Greg? – Oh, I'm sorry, I didn't know you were asleep.' His mother standing at the bedroom door, looking down at him; face captioned 'Concerned Parent'.

'Yeah,' he said, rubbing his eyes. 'Conked out.' 5.27 on the clock; radio playing in the kitchen.

'Are you OK?' his mother said. 'You seemed to be talking, or something. Thought you were on the phone.'

'Yeah – yeah,' he said. 'Strange dream.' He focused on her face, working out that she'd run out of things to say; was waiting for him to shovel words into the hole.

'It's OK. Be down – in two shakes.'

'Right. It's chops for tea – broccoli and baked potatoes.'

'Good,' and he sat up and swung his legs over the side, waited for the room to steady. His mother was still there, like an anxious child. 'I'm all right – you can go now,' like he was talking to some kind of retard.

'OK, then,' she said, and carried off her worry like a box of china; feet padding down the corridor.

In the kitchen they sat opposite each other, trying to talk.

'Good day?' his mother asked.

'So-so,' he said, touching the broccoli with his fork; trying to put together the pieces of his dream. Behind Suzie Marlowe was the huge black and yellow display board, with the scheduled times and destinations of trains. People scanning the screen, making decisions. That wasn't all; that wasn't everything, because all the times were the same, as though a dozen trains were going to crowd the four platforms at exactly the same time.

The great dark screen in the booking hall was flashing 12.09.

'Penny for them?' his mother said, looking across at him, right eyebrow raised.

'Had this – I dunno – weird dream – when you came up.' He looked down and stuck his fork into the baked potato. 'Just a jumble of stuff.'

Her face relaxed; she tried a smile. 'Always the way –
Don't know where the mind gets all the – the rubbish
– we dream about.'

He looked at her carefully. It was like every
conversation ended in a cul-de-sac. Like you started
something and there you were, at the terminus.

Her face had a worn, bleached look. As though all
the colours had been washed out. Her eyes were like
blue glass at the bottom of a pool.

'Maybe,' he said, and sawed the potato in half; looked
for the tub of margarine.

'Your father is in Birmingham,' she said.

'Yeah?' he grunted.

'Looking at the accounts – some big chemical firm.
Staying overnight.'

'Yes?' He took a shaving of margarine. He said: 'Does
"12.09" mean anything to you? Are those numbers –
or –' he considered: 'maybe it could be a date or
something – like the twelfth of the ninth?'

He didn't get any further, because she seemed to
gasp, pushed her chair back and got up from the table,
turning away with her left hand in front of her face.

'Are you all right?' he said, knife and fork frozen in
mid-air.

She shook her head and reached for a tissue. Blew
her nose, and turned towards him, suddenly fierce,

suddenly fully alive: 'Why do you do this to me?' she said. 'Why – why do you want to torture me – like this – about – about everything that happened. Those years ago. It's not fair, Greg. Simply, not fair.' And she turned away and looked out of the window.

He placed his knife and fork on either side of his plate, said to her back: 'Don't know what you're—'

'Yes, you do,' she said, her finger stabbing the air, her voice rising. 'You do know what I'm talking about – what all this –' and she broke off. 'I know you blame me, Greg – I've always known that – there's nothing I can do about that – but, why do you pretend you don't know that the twelfth – September the twelfth – was – Sarah's birthday.'

A fierce stare into his eyes. 'It was then, it is now.'

Ten

He shifted on his seat in the computer room, heard the anger in her voice; felt the heat of her glare. He turned back to the screen, fingers glancing over the keys:

We should have sorted all that stuff years ago. Maybe if we had, I wouldn't be sitting here, trying to tell my story, hiding away from the police and whatever else is out there.

Sarah was dead but we'd never been able to talk about it. My sister looked at us every time we went up the stairs but we weren't able to look at each other, except when we were chucking rocks, scoring points.

Even now, I feel angry about how the tone changed that day. It was like my mother was telling me that I didn't have any feelings about my dead sister. Maybe my mother thought that I had made up the dream in order to get a rise out of her. Something like that.

The next day? – Inderjit didn't show. It was the Friday before half term, and there was just a blank space in Maths, period two. He spent the hour working out an action plan to soothe Jordan – all the while fending off the stupid comments from Sheetal and Davindar; ignoring Fraser and Wiseman.

There had been no explanation for Inderjit's absence. Jordan grunted when he turned in the plan and muttered: 'Might have to cope on your own for a week or two.'

Thanks, he thought, looking at the figures he'd picked up from Inderjit. Wondered what the point of it all was.

Twenty-four hours later, and Suli was on the line. Voice like an express train. From a call box.

'No credit,' he said. 'Down your way, man, with Dilshad. Going to the ten-pin. Wanna come?'

And he thought, Yeah, why not? So he ran some water over his face, pulled on his black jeans, and tugged the laces on his trainers. 'Going bowling,' he said to his parents. 'With Suli and that. Dilshad.'

His father had looked up from his crossword and his mother simply said: 'That's OK, John? If Greg goes out with his friends?' The harsh words of Thursday night just so much small talk.

His father said: 'When will you be back?' Like Greg was a magician or something. Could predict how long the bowling would last.

'Hour and a half? Not late.'

And his father had turned back to his paper; his mother giving a watery smile, saying, 'OK, dear.'

He met Suli and Dilshad outside the ten-pin. Dilshad holding a spread of cod and chips; Suli swallowing from a can.

'All right?' Greg had said. 'Been waiting long?'

'Yeah, man,' said Suli. 'About forever,' allowing a smile to widen his face. 'Gotta wait for fishface here to finish.'

'Take a chip,' Dilshad said, offering Greg the mess of food.

'Aw right?' said Suli, pushing his shoulder, lightly. 'Dint wan to see you fade away. With no mates and that.'

The evening developed into a rhythm of turn-taking and rivalry, with Dilshad punching in the scores. And as Greg watched the fall of pins, so Inderjit's voice came back to him, like an irritating tune. 'There's something out there that's making these people sick. I need to find out what it is.'

He watched Suli fit his fingers into the holes, lifting

the ball on to his left hand whilst staring down the lane.

'Take your time,' Greg called out.

Suli turned, grinning. 'Can't catch me out like that,' he said. 'I'm focused.'

Catch the frame right, hit the first pin head on and the others were blown away. Send an off centre ball and you'd be lucky to hit a couple.

Is that what Inderjit figured?

Suli made his run and released the ball, standing up to watch its line.

Inderjit thought that something out there had hit the population like a bowling ball and scattered a whole cluster of lives. All you needed to do was work out the ball that was doing the damage.

That's if she was right about the figures.

He watched a crate lower a new triangle at the end of their lane.

'Your turn, Greg,' said Dilshad. 'Need a single strike and you'll win tonight's star prize.'

He collected his ball, slotted his fingers and imagined the path leading to the centre of the pins.

Plot the occurrence of disease – using an Ordnance Survey map – and you'd have a clear pattern staring you in the face. You'd see at a glance whether Inderjit's statistics were horse manure or meant something else.

'Come on, Greg,' said Suli, touching his shoulder. 'You're not launching a missile from Cape Canaveral.'

'Yeah, right,' he'd said. Took a couple of steps and let the ball roll in a diagonal that dropped it securely into the gully.

'Don't believe it,' Dilshad said. 'The Gretford bowling champeen blows a gasket.'

'Yeah – I wasn't thinking,' he said, turning round. 'Got my mind on other stuff.'

'Inderjit Sandhu,' said Suli, pulling on his bottle.

'Nah, nothing like that,' he said. But suddenly the bowling, the result, seemed pointless. He needed to get back and spread out the map; take a look.

Which was how he got to discard his last two attempts. Head full of other stuff.

He turned away from the lane and gave Dilshad a high five. 'Well done, my man,' he said. 'Seems that I lucked out. A worthy winner.'

''s nothing,' Dilshad said. 'Just takes the meeting of chance and genius –'

'Yeah,' said Suli, pulling on his jacket, 'collision with a star plonker, more like.' Looking across at Greg, his palms spread.

'Yeah,' he said, smiling. 'You might be right this one time.'

Eleven

The next morning, as the bells clanged from the church on the corner, he reached for the maths file in his bag. Pulled out the pages that Inderjit had downloaded. Leukaemia stats in the Oxfordshire Health Region. Pages of figures. Every town, village and hamlet listed on the spreadsheet.

He went down the corridor to the bookcase and pulled out the map for Gretford and District; had it half open before he'd passed back into his room.

His eye picked out the snaking red of the A14; a thick ribbon running across the bottom fifth of the sheet. Hindlip – where Inderjit lived – a couple of centimetres south, over on the left-hand side. A dozen miles from Gretford. Cycled out there a few times with Suli. No big deal.

He looked back at Inderjit's list. What it didn't show were individual pockets, hot spots. You could draw a big circle around Hindlip – note the villages within the circumference and then calculate the amount of disease that occurred. But that would assume a pattern of sickness with Hindlip as the centre. Draw four circles, north, south, east and west, with Hindlip in the middle and you'd get four sets of information, snapshots of adjacent land.

List the villages and feed the information on to a spreadsheet and that would reveal whether Hindlip was a statistical freak or whether there was something else, something going on out there.

He didn't get that far with the compasses – drew a couple of ten-centimetre circles when he heard a cough and his father was standing in the doorway.

'Not my map, is it?' he said. 'You didn't pick that up from the b-b-b-bookcase on the landing, did you, Greg?'

'Essential work, Dad,' he said. 'Major school project.' And then: 'Like you always want me to do so well.'

His father skirted the sheet and went over to the desk. Pulled a chair back and sat down. 'Have you developed some, I don't know – some attitude p-p-p-problem? Is that what this is all about?' And he gestured at the open map, the scattered data.

'Nope, this is a bit of maths research. Important stuff, Dad. Oh, and yes, it is your map. And yes, I did swipe it from along the corridor. And yes, I—'

'D-D-Don't talk to me like that,' his father said. 'End of Year 10 and you're wh-wh-what – involved in some squalid fight. Placed on r-r-r-report. And then your mother tells me about some st-stupid – comment you made – three days ago – about – Sarah? –' He stopped, took off his glasses and pinched the bridge of his nose.

'You've got that the wrong way round, Dad,' Greg said.

'But, you did make some comment about Sarah's birthday. That's true, isn't it?' he said. 'Some – c-c-careless – remark – That's so, isn't it?'

'No – not like you have it. It's not like that.'

'I'm going back to B-B-B-Birmingham. Early in the morning. I'll be there for most of this week. During that time, I don't w-want you out of the house – unaccompanied.'

Greg looked down. Saw the roads and railways. The splashes of colour.

'Aren't we – look, Dad, I'm fifteen. Not – not five. A bit—'

'—too old for this kind of thing? M-M-Maybe. But the downturn in your behaviour has – has – got to stop. So, you'll stay put. Understand?' He stood up and went the door. 'And if this week's a – OK – we can – relax the routine.'

'Dad,' he said, grabbing the last few seconds of self-control. 'It's half term. You expect me to stay indoors? For the complete week?'

'Yes,' his father said, finally. 'Exactly what I want,' – and then he was gone. His slippered feet padding along the corridor; fading away as he went down the stairs.

That was the last time Greg saw him.

Twelve

He waited for the coach to pass and then pushed off down the Melton Road, changing up and rapidly getting into the rhythm that would carry him half way across the county.

When his father had gone, Greg stretched out on his bed and stared up at the ceiling. Allowed the whole baggage-train to travel across the cracked white screen. The long-dead face of his sister peering round every bend in the road.

And yet it wasn't Sarah who'd prompted the ride, nor Suli, who had phoned that next afternoon, the Monday of half term; wanting to know whether he'd like to join him and Dilshad down the Silver Screen, for the new animation.

'Busy – but thanks,' he said and avoided mentioning the grounding. He went back upstairs, ignoring the query from his mother about whether he'd like a cup of tea. Or not.

It was because there was nothing else to do – no TV worth watching, no DVDs to see, no music to play or books to read – that he returned once again to the pile of stats and the map draped across the floor at the foot of his table.

'This going to help?' he'd said to James Dean, and picked up his notebook; started to write down the list of villages in each of the four circles. 'This going to get us to the land of milk and honey?'

When he finished, he switched on his computer and loaded a spreadsheet; sat back and thought about which fields to use.

He worked on the figures, on and off, for the rest of the day, and it was gone eleven that night when he finished. His fingers felt sore and his eyes were heavy. At the back of his mind the sense that he had been wasting his time.

'Sandbagged, man,' he said to Dean, and rubbed his eyes. 'Time to take a dive.'

He awoke to the sound of the milkman outside. He eased himself back against the headboard; heard the map sliding off the bed; knew that the grey box in the corner contained the data that would answer Inderjit's question.

Ten minutes later, he stared into the screen, looked into the well of light amidst the surrounding darkness. There were four files, using the same fields. He'd labelled them alphabetically, with 'A' containing places north of Hindlip and reaching just south of Market Harborough. He pressed the keys, made the calculation. Twelve settlements with an average of .18 per cent of sickness over the period. Nothing.

East of Hindlip, looking at the villages that lapped the outskirts of Gretford, the average was down to .12.

Some wild goose chase. Not even making the regional average. A neat set of stats that pointed nowhere. Made Suli and Deadman's traffic survey sound interesting.

He rubbed his eyes and leaned back. It was ten past three on a Tuesday morning in half term. Around him eighty thousand people were just turning over to settle into the next stage of their sleep. Here he was messing around with figures in the hope that he'd find something significant.

He got up and pulled back the curtain; stared out over the orange lights on the far hill; the rows of streets with the industrial estate beyond.

He wondered whether Inderjit was awake, tucked up a dozen miles away. What was she thinking about? Her dying grandfather? Old friends from Leicester?

He went back to the computer; loaded the third file, zone 'C'.

South of Hindlip, the villages thinned out: .22 per cent. A shade over two people in every thousand. Slightly higher than the average but not exactly bucking the trend. Well within any margin of error.

'Last throw of the dice,' he said to Dean, loading the fourth file and looking at the long column that listed villages to the west of Hindlip, that touched the edge of the map.

'Should've done a sandwich survey,' he muttered, and pressed return.

.48 per cent.

Four hundred and eighty people getting leukaemia in every one hundred thousand. The school hall packed to overflowing. Three times the national average.

'Can't be,' he said, and sat up. Touched the keys, redid the calculation.

The same digits flashing up on the screen. The same numbers telling him that you were three times more likely to get the disease if you lived in Hindlip or in any of the settlements immediately to the west.

Not only that, he thought, looking down. Not only that, holding the OS map. You could predict the amount of disease in the settlements that were over the border in the next map of the series, in another health region.

You could forecast illness from the information he held in his hand.

He looked out into the dark; heard the rumble of the bowling ball, the crash of falling pins.

Thirteen

He turned left and went down the lane past the Young Offenders hostel. A solitary face staring out, giving him the finger. Over the stream and underneath the rail bridge.

Somewhere his father was still there, standing by his door, telling him that he wasn't to leave the house 'unaccompanied'. He thought of that when he caught sight of the guy at the window, just back then. Like Dad wanted him electronically tagged or something.

His mother had come into his room at 8.30. She said: 'I have to go into school today. Probably tomorrow as well. Sort out the mess in my classroom. Be back by five. Could you make some tea? There's a spag bol in the freezer.'

'Yeah,' he said, rubbing his eyes. 'Yeah. Why not?'

'How do you feel?' she asked, holding the door handle. Standing next to the greyed-out James Dean; his left eyebrow raised; a slight curl to the lips.

'Fine,' Greg said.

'About going out −' she began.

'Yeah,' he said. 'I remember: "Not unaccompanied." That was it. Wasn't it?'

'Yes. It's just that − your father −'

'Spare it. I understand. What he said.'

A cloud of doubt shadowing her face. And then: 'Well, I'll be back by five. At the latest. See you then.'

He turned left at the junction west of Galtley, passing the old war memorial, beside the road leading to the landfill; saw the cloud of gulls plunging into the tiers of junk.

The rain started in the long curve to Stanton. The first heavy drops touching his face at the same moment he felt the pull of the front wheel; the rough-ride of the flat tyre.

He was soaked by the time he reached the cover of trees that lined the stream. Rain tapping the flattened leaves as he gutted the tyre on the footpath; the face on his watch splashed big.

He was bent over, turning the quick-release on the wheel when he felt the shift in light; heard the footfall behind him. Saw the black trousers and the scuffed boots.

'All right, son?' the policeman said. 'Bit of bother?'

Tall guy; body armour; carrying thirty pounds over

the odds. Face large and pasty beneath the flat cap. His mate in the squad car leaning forward, looking out. Watching.

Greg stood up, scratched an itch on his cheek, said: 'Yeah – that's about it. Got a flat.'

'Out for the day then, son? Come far?'

'Gretford,' he said, pulling a handkerchief from his pocket and rubbing his hands.

'And you're heading –'

'Hindlip.'

'Hindlip,' the copper said. 'Seeing a friend? Something like that?'

'Yeah,' Greg said. 'Something like that.'

'On your own then, son?' The copper looked along the path behind him. 'Haven't come with a mate. Or anything?'

Yeah, as if it's your business, thought Greg. 'Nah,' he said. 'On my own.'

'Right you are then,' the policeman said. 'Let you get on.' He looked up. 'Rain seems to be easing. For your ride.'

'Yeah,' he said, and watched the copper slope off back to the car, strap himself in and move on up the hill. Hand raised in silent salute.

'Yeah, right,' said Greg aloud and spat on to the damp earth.

Looked through the spokes of the front wheel and stared into the eyes of a small green frog, just in from the path, beneath a brush of grass.

Without bending, Greg could see the deformity; the strange splay of the fifth limb, ahead of the hind leg. And as he watched, so it crawled away into the undergrowth, pulled by the sound of the stream.

Fourteen

Hindlip was twenty minutes down the valley. Once he'd passed the first cluster of houses, he got off his bike and banged on the door of a terrace. Had time to count the pebbles stuck to the wall before an old guy looked out.

Blue eyes, thick moustache and a head of white hair. Had the voice to match. 'Yes?' he said, looking up at Greg. 'What do you want?'

'Sorry to bother you,' Greg said, pulling on a smile.

There was a dark corridor behind; a stink of dogs. The old guy checking his face like he'd appeared on *Crime Tonight*.

'Looking for a friend?' Greg said. 'Name of Inderjit Sandhu. Wondered if you knew where the Sandhu family live.'

More silence, the old guy bearing down on a knobbled walking-stick; face screwed into a knot. 'What do you want?' he said. And then: 'You don't come from round here.'

Greg said: 'I'm not here to rob you, mister. I've come over from Gretford to—'

'Gretford?' said the man. 'What you doing here, then?'

'Mister, I'm in a bit of a hurry. Sorry to bother you. I'll ask a bit further along,' and he pushed the bike up the narrow pavement. The old guy was still there, two minutes later: mouth open; stick at an angle.

There was a paper shop past the buttoned-up terraces, advertising ice cream and lottery tickets. The window stuffed with jars of boiled sweets.

Greg parked his bike against the glass, pushed the door back and heard the tinkle of the knocked bell.

A woman in a patterned dress appeared from a back room. 'Yes?' she said. 'Can I help you?'

'I'm looking for the Sandhu family. I think they live in the village, somewhere.'

'No Sandhu family I know of,' she said, hands flat against the counter, face unsmiling. 'An Indian family in Waverley Road, but they're the Virdees. Not Sandhus.'

'Oh,' he said, and rubbed some of the road grime from his face. Looked at the newspapers on the counter, the stacks of gum.

66

He glanced back at the woman: she hadn't moved; stock still, like some granite statue. Using words like they were a fiver each.

'It's just that I'm in the same class. At school. With Inderjit,' he said. 'Inderjit Sandhu. She lives here.' He looked back, through the glass of the door. 'Somewhere.'

'Inderjit,' the woman said, as if tasting the word. 'Bit broad round the beam? Needs to shift a few pounds?'

He didn't remember her like that. Not for a while, he thought. Just Inderjit Sandhu. 'I guess so,' he said.

'Mrs Virdee's granddaughter,' said the woman, sighing as though the effort was too great. 'The girl comes in here. Sometimes. Grandfather's quite ill.'

'Yes,' he said. 'That's right.' Realising that Virdee must be Inderjit's mother's name, before she got married.

The woman pointed to the door, to the churchyard beyond. 'Take the next turning. On the left. There's a "For Sale" sign on the corner. String of council houses. Virdees are half way down.'

She watched his face; checked the reaction. He wondered whether he should thank her and head off under the tinkling bell. Imagined tapping on a string of houses. Repeating the question.

She said: 'One second: I'll tell you the number.' And

she pulled a large delivery book from a shelf beneath the counter; turned to the back; flipped a few pages.

'Twenty-three Waverley. Half way down. On the right.'

'Thanks,' he said, turning away. 'That's helpful.'

'You're welcome,' she said and stood watching as he pulled back the door, went out and mounted his bike. Followed the shifts of his stiff-legged climb up the hill.

At the top, by the church, he saw the Waverley turning. There was a kid on the wall opposite; eight or nine with baggy trousers and a spread of untidy hair. A woman with a walking frame pottering about her garden on the nearside.

There was a green Toyota parked on the verge, outside twenty-three. The roof dulled by the sun; a split through the rear number plate. The house was one half of a semi; part redbrick, part a scattering of pebbles.

He left his bike on the lawn and went up the slight incline to the door. Pushed the bell a couple of times and waited. Looked out over the village.

'Yes?' said a voice behind him. 'Can I help you?'

A woman in her forties; dressed in a blue Punjabi suit. Hair parted in the middle and tied behind; old acne scars on her cheeks.

'Yeah,' he said. 'I've come to see Inderjit. I'm at school. In Maths. She—'

'*Kaun hai?*' from down the corridor.

The woman turned: '*Koi Inderjit lai hai,*' she said and faced Greg again, rubbing her left eye with her forefinger. 'She's not here,' she said. 'Gone out. I'm sorry.'

And the door was pushed to before he had time to figure out that the conversation was over. Just an expanse of white and the movement of a net curtain behind the glass.

On his way there, he'd rehearsed the moment when the door opened and he explained his mission. None of the scenes had the door opening and closing in under twenty seconds; him rooted to the path; face a blank.

He hauled his bike to the upright and slowly turned it round, hoping that the door would open and Mrs Sandhu would relent and invite him back. She'd apologise for her abruptness; excuse it on the sickness of her dad. Something like that.

But when he glanced back, the windows blinked in the sun and the door stayed shut.

At the junction, the kid on the wall shifted position, said: 'Looking for the Paki?'

Greg shrugged: 'Wanted to see Inderjit Sandhu. Lives back there.'

'Yeah,' said the kid, shaking hair out of his eyes. 'That's the one. Gone down the shop.'

'Right,' Greg said. 'Where's that?'

'Down there,' he said, indicating with a nod of the head. 'Just past the old garage. On the right.'

'I'll have a look,' said Greg.

But she wasn't there; not hiding by the frozen food or tucked away beside the detergents. There were a couple of kids pointing to a jar of sweets and two women chatting, but the place was small, dark – and empty of his Indian classmate.

'Want any help?' said a man in a white coat, carrying a box of soup cans.

'No,' he said. 'Just looking,' and left soon after, rubbing his eyes in the sudden sunlight.

Two minutes later, as he neared the church, he saw her in the graveyard, watching him from a seat pushed against the church wall. She was sprawled up against the corner, like a doll that had been chucked aside.

'I was looking for you,' he called out. 'Travelled over. From Gretford.'

'Yeah?' she said, watching him dismount, unmoving. 'I thought you might have come for your health.'

Fifteen

'Sorry – about the other day,' he said. 'You know – sad act and all that.' The words he'd been turning over in the ride across the county. The peace offering.

She looked at him, unmoving from her sprawl in the corner. Left leg pulled up and dark hair hanging loose. She waved her arm at him dismissively, bangles ringing in the air; gold glittering in the sunlight.

'And that sorts everything out?' she said. 'Makes everything better?'

'Nah,' he said. 'But I didn't mean anything. Not really.'

'So what was the need – when you were with Suzie Marlowe – to speak like that?'

He sat down at the far end and looked across the graveyard.

'People say things – don't mean them,' he said, and turned to look at her. 'Don't know why I said it.'

She looked down and pulled at a thread on her knee.

He felt backed into a corner. Heard again the slam of the front door in Waverley Road.

'Nannaji — my grandfather — is very sick. He's going into a hospice. This week —' and seeing the question on his face, 'A place where people die.'

'Sorry —'

She smiled. 'Seems to be your favourite word.'

'Where's this place?' he said.

'Gretford. Beyond the rugby club. Very nice — it's . . .'

They sat in silence. He watched the tousle-haired kid ease himself off the wall and head past the war memorial.

'I've done the figures,' Greg said, looking down. 'Checked everything.'

'What?' she said.

'You know — leukaemia stats. For the county.'

'And?'

He looked at her, leaning back with her head resting against one of the buttresses. 'You were right. That's all.' He stood up, looked out. 'This area — there's something making people sick. Your granddad — other people. Spreads into Leicestershire. Don't have the stats, but — you can work that out.'

She looked at him, and then resumed pulling at her knee. ''s a bit late. For Nannaji. He's got a couple of weeks. That's it. No more.'

'Let me show you,' he said.

'OK,' she said. 'OK.'

He pulled the map and file from his bag. Spread out the large sheet.

'Created a database. Plotted the figures. I've checked the increase of leukaemia over thirty years. In thirty-two villages.'

She looked at the numbers, said: 'Rise starts in '69. It's really steep and then tapers off. End of the eighties.' And then: 'So, what happened – between '68 and '69?'

'You tell me,' he said. 'Didn't have time to break everything down. Into age groups and that.'

She passed her hand across her face; as if wiping away a film of dirt. She looked away from him, over his shoulder, beyond the houses of the village, to the blue trees of the ridge.

'Inderjit –' he said.

'Nannaji used to work in the garage, over there,' she said, pointing. 'In the sixties. We'll have to talk to him. Before . . .'

'OK,' he said. 'If you think – Today?'

'He doesn't have many "todays",' she said. And then, touching his arm: 'Sorry. Shouldn't have said that. You better come back to the house.'

'Your mum – seemed – weren't that keen –'

'Yeah,' said Inderjit. 'Marriage is crap and her dad is

73

passing away. Trying to hold it together. You know. Come back, with me. It'll be OK.'

And so they went down the church path, crossed over the road by the memorial and trolled down Waverley to twenty-three.

'You let me do the talking,' said Inderjit. ''s no big deal.'

Sixteen

'This is Greg Price,' Inderjit said, introducing him to Mrs Sandhu. They were in the small kitchen, and Inderjit's mother was peeling potatoes.

'Yes?' she said. 'You found her then. In the village?'

'That's right, Mrs Sandhu –'

Her face bunched up and she said: '*Ithe kiyon enu leke aya ci? Teno patta nannaji theekh nahi hai.*'

Inderjit touched her mother's arm gently. 'It's all right, Mum,' she said. 'He's been helping me. I want him to see Nannaji. With me.'

Mrs Sandhu placed the peeler on the chopping board and wiped her hands on a towel. She said: 'What is this all about, Inderjit? Not your school work again?'

'We might know why your father got sick, Mrs Sandhu,' Greg said, stepping forward, so that he was next to the girl.

'And you know better than all the doctors and the consultants?' she said, leaning with one hand against the work surface. 'Two bright sparks from the local school suddenly know why my father is dying? It's not likely, Inderjit,' she said. 'Not all the doctors and consultants can puzzle out the answer.'

'It's—' began Inderjit.

'Mrs Sandhu,' said Greg quietly. 'We think that something happened. In 1968 or '69. That may have made your father ill.'

The woman looked down at the floor; wiped her hand across her forehead; looked at each of them. After a moment she said: 'When I was in junior school, living here, in this house, my father was taken into hospital. He had bronchial pneumonia. Nanniji was away, in India. Nannaji almost died. That would have been at the end of the sixties. Like you said.'

She paused and looked to her right, through the doorway that led into the dining room. 'He's sleeping at the moment,' she said. 'Nanniji is resting. If Nannaji is awake, you can speak with him. Five minutes. No more.' She went into the small dining room and a moment later Greg heard her quiet footsteps on the stairs.

Inderjit said: 'Mum's checking. See how Nannaji is. Come through.' And she led him into the lounge at the back of the house. Where they sat in silence. Listened to the low murmur of voices.

Greg looked over the garden, to the hedge at the bottom. Breathed in the hint of spices that carried through from the kitchen. A spray of lavender on the windowsill; a portrait of a turbaned figure over the fireplace. Right hand held up; a full beard against a yellow shirt.

And then? Mrs Sandhu came down the stairs; stood in the doorway and said: 'I've spoken to Nanniji, Inderjit. You can sit with Nannaji for five minutes. No more.'

'Thank you,' Inderjit said, standing.

'He might not wake up.'

The yellow light of the table lamp cast long shadows; filled the cheeks and eye sockets of the dying man, as though he were visibly sinking from the world, a dark sea lapping against his face.

Frail hair and wisps of beard on his chin. Everything looked too big for him – the striped pyjamas buttoned up to the neck; the spread of the double bed. His arms were stretched out, over the top of the duvet, as if he were trying to steady the world. And he slept with a slight wheeze that seemed to travel from somewhere deep inside. As though all the air was slowly escaping.

They sat on either side of the bed. Inderjit said: 'He's been given pain relief. Sleeps most of the day.'

'Yeah?' Greg said. Looked around the room: the dressing gown hanging from the door. A photograph of Mr and Mrs Virdee at some function. Years back. He looked strong and confident. A full beard, neatly combed; blue turban. A broad smile brightening his face.

Then, from out of the darkness, very faintly, so that Greg had to strain his ears, the old man said: '*Kaun hai?*'

''s Inderjit, Nannaji,' leaning forward, to touch his arm.

His eyes flickered and he looked up at the ceiling, as if trying to focus and then closed.

'I've brought my friend, Nannaji,' she said.

Greg watched the shallow breathing of the old man; noticed the khanda chain around his neck.

'Talk to him,' said Inderjit, softly.

Greg cleared his throat, felt awkward. 'Hello, Mr Virdee,' he said. 'We're here to ask you. About 1968. When you became ill.'

They waited in the twilight. Listened to the collision of sounds; kids playing in the street; a motorbike revving up; a saucepan being placed on the stove.

'He sleeps a lot,' said Inderjit. 'He may not have heard you.'

Her grandfather said: 'November.' The word easing out of his mouth like a sigh. 'In the garage.'

Inderjit placed her fingers into his hand; closed them lightly.

'He was a mechanic,' she said, looking across at Greg, and he remembered seeing the shuttered building as he cycled along the high street. A pair of rusting petrol pumps out the front and a faded sign advertising motor oil. Yet looking down, the old man was suddenly deeply asleep and it was almost as if Greg had imagined the wakened voice. Something dreamed.

But then Nannaji gave a great sigh and was immediately with them again, eyelids flickering, voice low. 'November '68,' he said. 'That night,' and immediately faded away; silence filling the dark.

They listened to the ticking of the clock. Waited for the small voice to grow loud; heard the cry 'Charlie!' outside and then Mr Virdee opened his eyes, pulled together the words: 'Working. Late. Jaguar. In the storm there was – explosion.' He paused, and slowly turned his head, looked at Inderjit. 'Creighton Wood,' he said. 'Big – flash.'

Greg leaned forward, trying to pick up the faint murmur of words.

'An explosion – in November?' Greg said, looking across at Inderjit.

'Yes. Yes,' she said.

But he was asleep again – eyes closed and the slow

rise and fall of his chest the only movement in that still room.

There was a sound outside and the door quietly opened. Mrs Sandhu said: 'You'll have to let him rest, Inderjit. He needs to look after his strength.'

'We're not—'

'Come on,' she said; 'he needs to sleep.'

They got up quietly and turned towards the door.

Behind them, they heard his voice, low down, paper-thin. He said: 'Three days – soldiers. Rifles.'

Seventeen

'What was that about, my friend?' said Raff, those days later. Sitting in Raff's lounge, with the borrowed sleeping bag folded in the corner; Greg's empty bag and the folder of notes parked on the side table. 'The flash in a winter's storm: the dream of a dying man?'

That's what he'd puzzled over, half an hour later, as he freewheeled down the slope towards Stanton. Just bits and pieces pulled out of the dark. Like some kind of strange lucky-dip at the fair. Bits and pieces.

They'd left the room and stood on the landing whilst Mrs Sandhu had eased the door to; followed her careful tread down the stairs.

He sat with Inderjit in the lounge for a quarter of an hour; both dazed, both still waiting for the voice to speak in the yellow light. And later, when the silence grew loud, they tried to pick up the fragments of conversation, the scraps of words and phrases that stuttered like an old car in winter.

'Thanks for coming,' Inderjit said, at last. 'Doing the work. Trying to help.'

He looked across at her, at the downturn of her eyes, her trembling lips; the way she sat with her fingers threaded; sunlight touching the red in her hair. He wanted to spread the map and say, 'Let's find the wood, Inderjit, see how far it is,' but – what was the point? It wasn't going to give strength to the dying; stop the slow, wheezing death of the old man.

'I'll think about what Nannaji said. What he told us,' she said.

'Yeah,' he said, reaching for his phone. 'You can have my email address and mobile number.'

And that was it. He'd been in the house scarcely a half hour and yet there he was, at ten to twelve, heading for the road.

'Thanks,' said Inderjit, one hand on the rusted gate. 'For cycling over and that.'

''s OK,' he shrugged. And then, as he waited at the kerb, 'See you.'

Through Stanton and then the slow climb along the side of the hill, before the drop into the valley – to the stream and the footpath trailing into the trees beyond. Where he'd sorted the tyre, met the police, looked at the frog.

He stopped at a passing point, opposite an old hay barn, and pulled the map from his bag. Looked at the lower section, below the fold; seeking out the green square that marked Creighton Wood. He followed the yellow road that connected Hindlip with Stanton and saw the long straggling wood rising up from the valley ahead. There was the footpath that followed the line of the stream. And beyond? The spread of brown contours; the zig-zag of power lines; dots marking a Roman road. Nothing to indicate the site of some explosion, thirty years before.

At the bottom of the valley, where he'd sheltered from the rain and stripped the inner tube, he swung to the left, and took the path beside the line of sycamores. He could hear the trickle of water falling beyond the grass and then he entered the shade of trees and the world became flecked with light.

The wood swung to the left, keeping to the slope of the hill, and the footpath went on, into the sunlight, past squares of spring wheat. The path was poorly used, he could see. Even in June, the grass was reclaiming the beaten earth and the only prints he saw were animal tracks. No scuff marks of walkers or mountain bikers.

With the wood a mile back, he was about to turn around when he saw, over to his right, beyond the shoulder of the hill and arising from an ocean of bleached grass, the square of a flatroofed building. Maybe a quarter of a mile away, over the stream and across a wire fence.

Single storey; brick built, with a concrete lintel over the door. Like a bungalow with the roof taken off, he thought, and brought his bike to a halt; checked the map.

He could tell from the spacing of the contours where he was, but there was no tiny square that indicated a building in the wasteland beyond.

'Join the sad acts,' said Greg, snorting, as he swung his leg over the saddle and wheeled his bike to the side of the path; splashed through the water and dropped it over the fence.

There was no one around. Had a look-see, left and right, but the field was empty. Just a wide open space and grass gone to seed. Knee-high and bent this way and that.

It was a shade after one and I dropped the bike after a few metres. I thought no one would wander off the track and take it.

The ground was pretty uneven, like it had never been tilled or whatever. It took me a good fifteen minutes to get to where I could squint at the lump of red brick on the far hillside. Even from three hundred metres it looked abandoned. The windows were a shiny blank and the walls were covered with lichen.

There was a ragged line of hawthorn ahead, and that was as far as he got. Couple of metres on the other side and the ground dropped away, ten metres down on to a broken track that opened up right and left. A hundred metres across – a great crevasse.

Old iron ore workings, he thought.

And as he stood there, staring across the scar towards the building, he wondered if anything fitted – the explosion those years before; the sickness in this part of the county; the great moat gouged out of the earth.

The sun was getting into its stride by then but there was something else, something deeper, more human – coming at him from the right, beyond the curve of the hill.

He didn't run or anything, when he saw the four-by-four. Didn't occur to him that there was anything to run away from. But it came bumping and snarling at speed, the long grass flattened in its wake.

It stopped ten metres away and for a few moments, nothing happened. The sun bounced off the screen so that all he could see were clouds passing; all he could hear was the slow breathing of the engine.

Then the window slid down and a woman with a large face and green shirt looked out. 'Can I help you?' she said. Brown hair tucked behind in a clip; a hint of lipstick. Like someone behind the ticket counter at a railway station. Except the voice was sharp, clear, cultured.

'No,' he said. 'Just looking.'

The woman pulled on the handbrake, dropped the gear into neutral. 'This is private property, you know. You shouldn't be here.'

'Yeah?' he said, bending down to pluck a blade of grass. Something to chew on.

He heard a murmur from inside, the woman's head turned to her left. Listening to an invisible accomplice, a soft-voiced stranger; and then there was a click and the passenger door opened.

He was a tall man, with light grey hair, cut short and brushed forward. Dark blue eyes and deep plough lines across his forehead. Amusement seemed to hover about his mouth, his eyes. Like he found the behaviour of the known world some kind of joke.

'Hi there – what are you doing so far off the beaten track?' A soft, northern voice. Hitting the pronoun so that it seemed to hang in the air long after the sentence had passed.

'Having a look,' Greg said. 'All right?'

The man smiled, stood next to him, looked out across the great scar. 'Bit of a mess,' he said.

'Eh?' Greg said, off-balance.

'The ditch.' Nodding down. 'Quarry workings.' He looked at Greg. 'Steel company used tracked vehicles with drag lines – to quarry the iron ore.'

Vee-icles, he said, pushing the first syllable; stretching his mouth wide.

'I know I'll sound like a bit of a – kill-joy,' he said, 'but this *is* private property. You're not supposed to be here.' And then, looking back down the slope; gesturing with his arm: 'All private. From that fence there.'

'Yeah?' Greg said. 'Didn't catch the sign. Back there.'

The man smiled. 'It's a pain,' he said. 'But – as Margaret said, you're trespassing – and I will have to ask you to return – to the public right of way.' He'd clipped the 'g' on 'trespassing'; had thrown all the weight on to the second syllable. TresPASSin, he'd said.

'Yeah?'

'Yes, 'fraid so.'

The guy allowed the silence to build, so that Greg became aware of the quiet murmur of the engine, the whisper of wind through the grass. The clear blue eyes and mild smile.

He was just putting together his farewell, face-saving

line, when there was a sudden commotion inside the vehicle.

'Situation update, Echo One.'

Eighteen

'No peace for the wicked,' the man had said, nodding towards the car. 'So – you'll make your way back to the footpath and we'll all be happy bunnies.' He paused and looked over Greg's shoulder, as if contemplating some figure approaching from behind. His eyes flicked back, studied Greg's face; calm, curious.

Greg shrugged his shoulders. Gave up. Said: 'OK mister. You win,' and pulled the piece of grass from the corner of his mouth; chucked it aside, as if to say, 'What the hell?'

He'd started to move away, to walk down the slope, when a thought struck him, so that he turned back and said: 'You're the landowner – right?'

Nothing from the guy for a second. A raised eyebrow. 'I work for the landowner,' he said eventually. 'He's – the boss.'

'See you, then,' said Greg and turned away, heading

off down the hill, across the wasteland. He didn't look back – just focused on the thin line of the footpath in the distance, beneath the overhang of trees. Imagined the thoughtful face and soft smile watching his progress through the grass.

Ninety minutes later and he was back in the kitchen, levering the top off an old ice-cream tub containing bolognaise sauce. Half past two and there was no message from his mother; nothing to suggest that she'd called home, to see how he was getting on.

Just him and Jimmy Dean. And the old picture of Sarah at the top of the stairs.

He placed the tub in the microwave; tapped in forty and pressed defrost. Listened to the slow whine of the machine.

He dismissed the guy in the off-road; placed it to one side as a problem that could wait. Switched his attention back to Hindlip. Who else was living in the village at the time of the explosion in November '68? Who else was still alive who could remember the soldiers, 'with rifles'?

He thought of the slate roofs and the war memorial and the unhelpful faces. The way he'd had to drag the information out of the woman in the paper shop; the old guy leaning out and staring after him as he'd walked away. The white door closed in his face.

A dark room and a dying man.

Ten minutes later and he was chaining his bike to the railings by the library; pulling his bag free. Made his way through the turnstile and into the reference section. Waited at the desk for the librarian to finish explaining the catalogue system to an old woman who needed to know about 'genealogy'.

Greg scanned the noticeboard; noted the flyers for support groups, folk clubs, ramblers. Read about domestic violence and Neighbourhood Watch. Was half way through a sheet advertising soil analysis when the librarian said: 'Yes? Can I help you?'

He drew a deep breath, made his play – drew another blank.

'I'm sorry, but we don't keep that information. Not here. You'd have to try the county archive, down at Delapre Abbey in Northampton. They might be able to help you.'

A large woman with an accent like washed gravel. Glaswegian vowels and consonants tangled like bramble.

'So – there's no way I can compare – you know – the names of people living in Hindlip now with the names of the – ah – residents – thirty years ago?'

'I'm sorry, dear,' she said, blue eyes looking at him with a hint of distress. 'But as I said, you'd need the old electoral register. To make the comparison. We don't keep that information. Not here.'

'Oh.' Listening to the echo of the slammed door; hearing that soft northern voice telling him he was 'trespassing'.

'Are you looking for anyone in particular?' the librarian said, encouragingly, trying to fathom what he was after.

'Nah,' he said. 'Just need to find out who was hanging around – living in the village then and now. School project.'

'Ah,' she said, 'then I'm sorry I can't be of any help.'

He turned away, stepped past a guy who was pulling a copy of the *Gretford Argus* from a rack.

He left his bike at the library and walked down the high street, past the market traders; intent on dropping into Soundz to check out the NeuJazz stack.

Beyond the wholefood restaurant, the crowd started to thicken; kids from different schools hanging around; delivery vans unloading; music banging out from the computer shop by the Thistle.

As he got level with the chemist, there was a familiar shout from the other side of the street: 'Greg!' and at the same time, as his eyes scanned the crowd, his legs walked into an obstacle and the ground smacked into his face.

A woman with a small child said sharply, 'Watch – what you're doing!' and as he struggled to his feet, so he saw the back of a denim jacket moving away, by the Baptist church; a neck marked with spots; dirty brown hair: Wiseman. On the other side, hand raised in recognition, Carl Fraser, sitting on the low wall of the council flowerbeds. Sly smile; tab tucked in the corner of his mouth; eyes narrowed against the smoke.

'How're yuh doin'?' he seemed to say. 'Nice trip?'

Nineteen

It took him a couple of seconds to get himself together: to pick up his bag and feel the graze on his forehead. He dusted his jeans and headed for where laughing boy was perched.

'Big joke,' Greg said. 'A real gut-buster.'

'Glad you thought so,' Fraser said, spitting into the flowerbed.

'You trying to say something, Fraser?' he said. 'Is that what this is all about?'

'Just having a ciggie, mate,' looking up through the smoke. 'Minding my own business.' He took the cigarette out of his mouth, held it with three fingers, head tilted to one side. 'You still going out with that – what'shername? Indershite?'

Greg took a step closer, leaned into Fraser's face: 'That's right, dogbreath,' he said. 'That's the one,' tapping him on the chest, threatening to tip him backwards. 'See you at the party. We can talk then.'

In the music shop, he picked up a set of earphones and plugged into Sonja Marks. Let his breathing return to normal; let a cascade of notes pour down in a blue shower. He looked out over the high street and watched Wiseman chatting to Fraser, over by the newspaper seller. Ignored the ache in his forehead; thought about Hindlip.

'There ain't no way but back,' sang the vocalist. 'Ain't no way.'

Outside, the old guy on the corner was yelling, '*Argus*! Get yer *Argus*! *Argus*!'

He let the song ripple to the end, hung the earphones on the hook and headed out into the three o'clock sun. There were dark patches on the other side, where the morning's rain hadn't dried. Small kids on skateboards; the sweet stink of fat and onions from the burger stall; heels tap-tapping back to the bike stand.

Newspapers carry stories, he thought. Someone must have written up an account of the explosion those years ago. The trick was to find it.

He followed another cyclist up the hill past the psychiatric hospital and after he'd locked his bike to a post, went through the swing doors of the *Gretford Argus* and stood at reception. Waited for a white guy in a too-big suit to finish on the phone, to look up and say, 'Can I help you?'

He said: 'Do you have a collection of back issues? Like for November and December 1968?'

The guy sat looking up for a moment and Greg thought he hadn't heard right, that he'd have to go through the explanation again; that he hadn't used the right words or that his clothes were the wrong colour. Or something. There was a badge on the scrawny guy's shirt pocket – it said: 'Stuart Fitton'.

He said: 'One moment, please,' a frown creasing his forehead, and he lifted the phone; punched three numbers; waited.

'Hello, Meera?' he said. 'Right – sorry to bother you – yes – it's – I know – third time – I've got a request to look at the archive. I know that – one second –' and he said to Greg, 'What is the nature of your enquiry?'

'I'm doing a project for school. On – ah – unemployment.'

Another pause and the guy spoke into the receiver: 'School student researching unemployment. Yeah – I know.' He put his hand over the mouthpiece. 'We really need a reference from your headteacher, something like that. My colleague is just checking. Seeing what we can do.'

'Thanks,' he said and stuffed his hands into his

pockets; turned round and looked at the photographs on the far wall; four guys in suits with smiles like bank notes.

The analogue clock to his right inched forward another click. 3.22 it said. His mother would be packing up her stuff; sticking boxes in the boot. Another minute crept past and a woman came down the stairs on the far side and dropped a magazine into the tray on the receptionist's desk.

'OK, Stuart?' she said, smiling. All blue skirt and white blouse.

Fifteen miles away the old guy would be wheezing in his twilight room; Inderjit at his bedside; her hand holding his.

Behind him, the phone rang and the receptionist said: 'That's great. Thanks, Meera. I'll bring him along,' and replaced the receiver. 'You're in luck,' he said, smiling. 'The boss is out and my colleague has just made an executive decision.'

First break in a week, Greg thought. 'Thanks,' he said.

Through the double doors and ten metres down a narrow corridor and he was led into a large open area of desks and space dividers. People in conversation, on the phone, tapping on keyboards.

'This way,' Stuart said, leading him through another entrance. They went up a flight of stairs and then stood before a door with the single word 'Records' printed in white on a black surround.

Inside, there was an Asian woman using a keyboard; fingers a mess of gold and the glare from the screen throwing text on to her glasses.

'One second,' she said. And then, looking at him, said: 'How can I help you?'

'Doing research,' he said. 'For a maths project. Need to find out about late November, early December. 1968.'

'I'll leave you then,' said Stuart, and touched his arm.

'Oh?' said the woman, moving a notebook to one side, and removing her glasses: 'Why the end of '68? What was going on then?'

Her name was Meera Dhar. He could work out that much from the name printed on the card mounted at the front of her desk.

He shrugged: 'I've got information about unemployment and I just want to see how the news was being covered. In the *Argus*.'

'OK,' she said. 'Copies of the papers for those weeks will be delivered to the meeting room –' she indicated another door. 'I can let you have forty-five minutes, but that's it.'

'OK,' he said. 'Thanks.'

She got up and led the way across her office, the hem of her sari just touching the floor; her dark hair held by a slide. Reminded him of Inderjit. Except there was no hint of red in this woman's hair. Just touches of white, like strands of steel. At the open door she turned and pointed to a grey box high up in the far corner. 'CCTV,' she said; 'just so that you know.'

I didn't have any great expectations. I thought that I wouldn't find anything – or that the relevant story would have been removed from the pages. A neat square cut from the sheet, like you see in Hollywood films.

Inderjit's grandfather had mentioned a storm in November and an explosion over Creighton Wood, and I thought that if I started with the beginning of the month I could simply skim the front pages in the first instance, and then, if I found nothing, could check the other stuff inside.

I suppose nowadays, with computer technology and so forth, I would simply load up the back issues and do a regular search of key words – like 'explosion' and 'November' and '68', but none of those old copies were in electronic format, so it was simply a matter of turning pages; giving the occasional nod to the CCTV blinking in the corner.

After half an hour he'd drawn a blank. No record of an explosion. Not even news of storm damage. Certainly no holes had been scissored out. Just yellowing sheets, grey photographs; adverts for dog food and houses.

At five to four, Meera Dhar opened the door quietly and said: 'How're you doing?'

'Nothing much,' he said, turning a sheet.

'I can let you have another five minutes, but that's it,' she said.

'OK,' he said. 'Thanks.'

There were probably thirty seconds left on the counter when he picked up three paragraphs at the bottom of page five – on the issue of 21 November. Thursday's edition. It read:

Plane Crash

The Ministry of Defence confirmed yesterday that a Canberra bomber from RAF Wyton, Huntingdonshire, crashed near Stanton on Tuesday night. Fire crews from Gretford and Market Harborough attended the scene and the blaze was quickly brought under control. The MoD said the crew of two ejected safely.

Fire crews from Gretford . . .

Twenty

'That was it,' he said, that first evening in Raff's flat. 'A plane dropped out of the sky, cratered the ground. End of story.'

'Yeah?'

'But – I could see there had to be something else.'

Like Inderjit said. Something out there. He had known that, as he pushed through the late afternoon traffic. Pushed the pieces around as he pedalled down Southfield Avenue. Thought about the stack of leukaemia cases that had appeared from 1969; the sick guy who remembered an explosion late one night – who'd said there were soldiers in the neighbourhood. An area of the county that was so off-limits that he'd been questioned the first time he went there.

And the frog with five limbs that had crawled into the undergrowth.

It made his brain feel like marshmallow. Did it add

up to anything? Like a sheet of quadratic equations that Jordan used to set.

He thought about calling Suli or Dilshad, getting them to help with the jigsaw, but knew that neither of them would get beyond the fact he was working with the new girl. He could imagine Suli's face, twisted in amazement. 'You're doing what, man?' he'd say, taking a step back. 'You have to be joking, right?'

'Beyond a joke, innit,' Dilshad would say, taking another bite from a chocolate bar. 'Lost your mind, man.'

He didn't get back until just gone 4.30 but there was no sign of the red Peugeot out front; his mother must have been snagged by some hitch at school.

He filled the kettle and pulled the blue tin of dried spaghetti from the cupboard; went into the hall and checked for late afternoon phone calls. *Nada.* Nothing on his mobile either.

The kettle had long since boiled when he heard his mother drop her stuff on the porch – her face fragmented in the frosted glass as she fumbled for keys.

'Hi,' he said brightly, as she came into the house. 'Good day?'

'Ye-es,' she said. 'OK – how about you?'

'Oh – nothing. Quiet.'

He followed her down the hall, carrying her box of exercise books.

'Came home at lunchtime. You weren't here,' she said, dropping her bag on the table and picking up the post; flipping through the envelopes as he went over to switch on the kettle. 'So, where'd you go?' she said.

'Library,' he said. 'Needed to check the electoral register. Maths project.' He collected a pair of mugs from the tree by the microwave. 'Sorry,' he added. Trying for damage limitation.

She ran her nail under one of the envelopes; levered it open. 'What happened to your face?'

His hand reached up, felt the graze on his forehead. 'Front wheel ran along the kerb,' he said. 'Came off.'

'Have you seen Carl Fraser again?' Looking across at him. 'Is this round two?'

'You've lost me,' he said, turning away.

She dropped a bill on the table and took off her jacket. 'What I mean to say—'

'No,' he said. 'I have not had another fight with Carl Fraser – or with anyone else.'

'Greg – I don't want to turn this house into a prison, but—'

'Didn't think going to the library – you know – counted,' he said. 'You can phone them, if you like. I spoke to the—'

She glanced down at the newspaper, scanned the front page. 'You didn't think to drop me a text or give me a call? Let me know your plans?'

Questions like bursts of machine-gun fire. Somewhere, in some other universe, he wanted to say – 'No, Mum, I wasn't able to tell you my plans because –' But he didn't even start. Couldn't find the words.

'Should have called you,' he said. 'Fouled up, there.' And then, as he poured water into the teapot. 'Spag bol is defrosted. When do you want to eat?'

After tea, after the small talk and pasta, he climbed the stairs to his room and switched on the computer; touched 'Mailshot'.

'*Hi Inderjit,*' he wrote, '*Maybe we could chase up some of the people who were around Hindlip in '68/69? Find out what they saw? The woman in the newsagent – she'd be worth asking.*

'*Checked some old copies of the* Argus *this p.m. An aircraft crashed on 19 November – near Stanton. Fits with your grandfather – about the explosion, over Creighton Wood.*'

He sat back and looked at the ceiling, glanced at James Dean staring down. Gaze like a question mark;

doubt flickering around his eyes; 'so what?' in the undone tie.

'So a lot,' Greg said, looking back at the screen.

The thing was, it wasn't just any old aircraft. The report mentioned a Canberra bomber. Military type. That might have some significance.

He moved the cursor up, added '*RAF*' ahead of '*aircraft*'. Just in case it rang a bell.

'*Difficult to get out atm,*' he wrote, '*but could travel over.*'

He paused, then tapped out:

'*From your friend – Greg.*'

Clicked the send button and watched the cartoon wings carry it off, into the dark.

'We'll see,' he said to the silent Dean. 'Might be worth something.'

Thirty minutes later, as he lay, watching *Quatermass*, he heard the tumble of notes from the phone in the hall. His father calling from Birmingham. Providing an update; checking in.

He adjusted the sound with the remote and listened to his mother run through the stuff she'd taken off the walls in her classroom; the way she'd cleared out the stock cupboard. Nothing about an absent son. Except for one place where she said: 'No – working on some maths, I think. A school project – yes, yes, that's right.'

Keeping the temperature down; heat under control.

At ten o'clock, when he pulled back the lounge door to say he was going to hit the sack, it was to find his mother sorting through packs of 35mm film – the coffee table a mass of colour photographs: frozen images from a dozen holidays.

'What you doing?' he said, going over and picking up a gap-toothed shot of himself on a beach. He flipped it over: *Greg at Weymouth. Aug '95* it said in his mother's tidy script. He'd been six; Sarah elsewhere, aged two; a year to live.

'I'm looking for our holiday in Portreath,' his mother said. 'Mary Gibbons is going there. Thought she might like to see what it's like.'

'These are Weymouth,' he said, lifting another picture – his father asleep in a deckchair; sunglasses half off; *The Times* spread across his chest.

'Just got distracted,' she said. 'Always do.'

He reached down and picked up a packet from the box on the floor. '*Various, '95*' it said on the label; he pulled out the stack of twenty-four photos. They'd been taken over several months. There were a couple of Sarah playing in the sandpit in the garden; himself on his bike – it was still bright red from the shop; an uncertain wave as he pedalled past. Photographs from their weekend in the Peak District – his father carrying Sarah on his shoulders across a shallow river; himself feeding a gaggle of ducks and geese.

But he soon forgot about these when he came to three at the bottom. They'd been taken at some social event. The light was low and the photographer had used flash. The first was a picture of his father and two women from work. He was laughing at something one of them had said: head back, mouth open.

In the second, his father and the two women were still in the frame, but the centre of attention, the real subject of the shot, was a couple by the bar. A woman in her thirties holding a drink and deep in conversation with a tall guy with short grey-flecked hair. He was turned away from the camera, so that it was difficult to get a positive identification – and it was suddenly difficult to still the trembling in his hands.

When he turned to the last image, he knew who he was looking at. The woman was now out of the frame and the man had just turned to stare at the camera, his right hand half raised; his left holding a beer glass. A soft voice that said: 'You're trespassing.'

Twenty-one

'Who's that?' he said, turning to look down at his mother. 'At the community centre?' Handing the picture over.

She adjusted her glasses, took the photograph, leaned back on the sofa.

'Ah – that would be – Peter Bonnington. He was attached to some woman who worked with your father. Haven't seen him in years.' She returned the picture, went back to the mass of photographs on the table; her eyes scanning the images; not meeting his gaze.

'Right,' he said, quietly. 'Right,' and then, firing blindly, 'Think I saw him today.'

'Oh?' She looked at him quickly, the colour touching her cheek; alarm like lightning across her face. 'Where was that?' she said, turning away.

He considered, thought about his options. 'Oh, just in town.'

'Did he – did he see you? Say anything?' she said.

Her hand rubbing her cheek; a short glance.

'Nah – Mum – he doesn't know who I am. How could he?' And then, with just a light touch: 'Did you know him – well? Back then?'

'Just an acquaintance, Greg. Someone we saw socially – from time to time. And talking of which, I'd better pack this stuff up – head off upstairs.' She started to collect the array of photographs and place them back in their packets. Like she was suddenly in a hurry.

'OK, then,' he'd said. 'I'll see you in the morning.' And turned away, his mother's gaze following him to the door.

He lay awake for a long time; felt the texture of the grass beneath his feet; looked again at the grey-haired figure, with the quiet smile and steady blue eyes. Heard the pitch and roll of his words.

But that wasn't the main thing that lay like cast iron on his chest: it was the chance discovery of the photograph in the collection downstairs. No sooner had he collided with the guy in the middle of nowhere than he found his mother had known him in some past life. This wasn't just some gamekeeper working his patch but 'Peter Bonnington', the friend of someone his father knew.

He looked up at the ceiling, thought of the ten-pin two nights back; the friendship of Suli and Dilshad; the competition to make the highest score. Good mates, but he had other things on his mind now.

The light was grey, coming in at an odd angle. He felt disorientated, as though he'd woken in a strange bed, a changed room. It took him a few seconds to get his bearings. The poster of James Dean seemed to have fallen down, because his door was bare. His old dressing gown hanging from a hook; dark shadows falling where the computer sat.

Down the corridor, a woman was singing a kid's nursery rhyme, thin and wiry. The pianist gave the tune too much treble, so the accompaniment seemed to overwhelm the voice, bury it beneath the weight of notes.

He could hear the run of a skateboard in the corridor; the short rumble of wheels as someone pushed it back and forth from Sarah's old room, past the toilet, to the gap at the top of the stairs. The turn of the wheels muffled in the carpet; a kid's voice calling: 'Geg, Geg.'

And suddenly, he knew that he had to get up, get into the corridor and wrap his arms round his sister, hold her away from that dark flight.

'Sarah!' he called: 'Sarah – wait! – wait!'

His scream brought his mother into the room, the light snapped on, her face bent over his.

'It's OK, Greg,' she said. 'It's all right. You're all right.'

Her hands touching his shoulders. 'Just a dream,' she said. 'A dream.'

'Yeah – yeah,' Greg said and rubbed the back of his hand against his eyes, as if to wipe away the night, bring himself back to the present. He could feel sweat prickling in his hair; sticking his pyjamas to his skin. He leaned against the headboard; allowed the child's voice to fade.

His mother looked around the room and said quietly: 'What was it about?' A strand of hair fell across her cheek. 'You were calling Sarah's name.'

'Yeah,' he said. 'Nightmare. She was – here – outside – in the corridor. I – I tried to save her –'

His mother lightly touched his leg through the duvet. She said: 'I think you need to talk to Dr Stretton.'

'No – I'll be all right,' he said. 'Just a dream.'

She allowed the silence to settle; looked back at him, eyebrows raised.

'Not just a dream,' she said softly. 'It's happening again, isn't it? The nightmare, notes stuck to your monitor?' She stared around the room. 'Dr Stretton could give you something. Listen to you.'

'What – what d'you mean about the monitor?' Greg said, trying to look past her. 'What did you mean?'

'The kid's note left there, like a – a reminder?'

She got up and pulled the paper off the screen.

'Read that and tell me you don't need to talk to someone.'

It had been attached by a strip of tape; a piece of notepaper ripped from a book. Crude letters in a child's hand, scrawled in blue crayon. Couple of lines that said:

After the fall

what did you see?

Twenty-two

Days later and he was stuck in the computer room in the strange college. The place seemed deserted. The spiky-haired woman hadn't come back after the first week and now there was a thin guy in shirt and tie, stapling worksheets from a pile.

When Greg told Raff about the dream, about the note on the monitor, Raff had said slowly and deliberately: 'You talking jumbies there. Ghosts.' He hadn't smiled.

Greg said: 'Yeah. I know I was haunted. We all were.'

Raff touched his arm: 'Ghosts is just stuff that hasn't settled right.'

Back then? In Gretford? – He'd smiled at his mother's suggestion that he talk to someone. Leaning against the headboard and reading the rough words on the torn page. The irregular formation of letters, the ragged line. Some kid trying to tell him something.

He looked at Raff, said: 'You might as well know, just

in case it comes up or something – well – after my sister died, I used to sleep walk. Nothing too terrible. Wander around the house and that.'

'Yeah?'

'That's it. My counsellor once asked what I was looking for but I didn't know then.' He shrugged. 'Guess I was trying to make sense of what had happened – when I was a kid.'

When his mother left the room, he lay in the twilight. Looked over at James Dean and wondered, for the first time, whether he should give up the chase – forget all the stuff about the leukaemia and Inderjit's project. Since she arrived, everything seemed to have become turned around. Stuff he'd spent years forgetting was now hammering on the door. Like it was all really there, just waiting to stride on in and mess up his life.

'What d'you think, James?' he said.

But Dean just stared back, those quiet eyes saying, 'Your call, Greg. You know that, don't you?'

Which suggested there was some sort of choice; that he could forget about Inderjit and Hindlip and everything over on the west side. Like he could get off the train and carry on as if nothing had happened. Go back to throwing balls down the lanes and taking the michael out of Davindar and Sheetal.

Raff had said: 'Jumbies won't let go until they get what they came for.'

Which he'd known anyway, lying there in that half light. Looking at the crayoned words; hearing the rattle of the skateboard.

Later, at 2.20, he reached into his drawer and pulled out his mobile. Switched on a new SMS and tapped out a message:

'*Hi Indy,*' it said, '*B over 2morrow. B with u @ 11. Knock on doors. TB. Greg.*'

He checked the signal, pressed '*send*'.

His mother said: 'I'm going into school now. I'll give you a call at lunchtime.'

She was standing in the doorway, wearing jeans and a dark blue sweatshirt; hair tied back and a denim bag at her side. The clock said 9.10.

'OK,' he said.

'How do you feel? After last night? No more dreams?'

'No, no – it was OK. Just feel tired, that's all.'

'Oh – and Greg – about going out –'

'If I get the urge – I'll call you,' he said.

She looked at him for a moment, said, 'That's right. And if you get the urge to see Dr Stretton, then phone the surgery. Might be a good idea.'

'See you later,' he said.

'I'll be back by five. At the latest,' she said and walked off down the corridor. 'Do the washing-up, can you?'

The phone rang as he was standing by the sink, looking out over the garden, tea in his hand.

'Yeah,' he said.

'Is that Greg Price?' said a girl's voice.

'Yeah. Hello, Suzie. What can I do you for?'

'Don't get cheeky, Greg,' she said, the words rounded by a smile. 'Having a good half term?'

What was that supposed to mean? 'So-so. This and that.'

'Carl said he saw you yesterday.'

'Right. He was one half of a comedy twosome,' he said. 'I haven't stopped laughing.'

'That's good, isn't it?' she said. A microsecond of edge in the upturn of her voice.

'Hilarious,' he said.

'Anyhow loverboy, what I really called to find out was whether you're going to Catherine's party – on Saturday.' She paused and in the background, he could hear the TV. Some daytime game show; applause like static.

'Yeah,' he said. 'I think I might do that. Why do you

116

want to know?' Just a tad of pressure on the pronoun; a slight shift of emphasis.

'Nothing serious —' she laughed. 'Catherine's restricted to thirty people. Needs to check numbers. That's all.'

'OK,' he said. 'Now you know.'

'Thanks, Greg,' she said softly. 'I've missed you.'

'Yeah and me you. Bye,' he said, and put the receiver down. Went back into the kitchen and threw the remains of his tea down the sink.

Suzie Marlowe? He had no time for her now.

Twenty minutes later and he'd breasted the hill before Brassington; a few stray tufts of cloud and a breeze as soft as warm milk. In the drop down into the valley before Stanton, he looked across at the dark outline of Creighton Wood and the open wasteland in the distance. But there was no sign of a green four-by-four and there were no walkers on the footpath by the stream.

Inderjit's text had simply said: '*C u @ 11 war mem*' and he'd made good time from a late start, driving himself along the curves and slopes. Thinking of the doors that had to be knocked and the need to be up and out by four.

Yet when he'd made the main drag into Hindlip, past

the terraced houses and newsagent's, and had dismounted by the church, there was no sign of the girl. The steps by the memorial were bare and no one sat on the bench in the churchyard.

It was just gone eleven and he leaned against the graveyard wall. On his phone he tapped out: '*Where r u?*' and had barely sent the message when he heard footsteps behind and Inderjit was looking down: 'I'm here,' she said. 'What kept you?'

Twenty-three

'How's your grandfather? he said.

She sat on the wall, feet hanging against the stonework. 'Going into the hospice. Friday.'

'Oh.' The silence expanding to fill the space. 'Sorry.'

'I know,' she said. Her hand touching his shoulder. 'It's –'

'Do you want to go ahead –' he said, waving at the houses on the other side. 'Banging doors?'

'Yeah,' she said. 'Do me some good.' She wiped her nose. 'Tell me about the *Argus*.'

'Oh – RAF plane crashed near Stanton on 19th November, 1968. That's it. Crew ejected. Fire put out.'

'Nothing else?'

'Nope – didn't give me long to look.'

'Like, you know, what Nannaji said about the explosion –?'

'Yeah, but nothing about soldiers or that. We need to

119

– it would help if there was someone else round here
from then. We could check with.'

'I can't ask Mum, at the moment,' she said, looking
away. 'People she's friendly with.'

'The woman in the newsagent's – she'd know who's
been around –'

'OK,' she said; easing herself off the wall. She looked
at him and smiled. 'You're OK when you're not trying
so hard to be someone else,' she said.

They followed the path round the side of the church
wall and Greg locked his bike against a lamppost. The
woman in the newsagent's had been replaced by an
eighteen-year-old girl. All fair hair and slender fingers;
a T-shirt that said Job *Shift*. Smile as wide as the Pacific.

Greg said: 'We're doing some research. For a project?
Need to talk to people who've lived in the village – for
a bit. Do you know of anyone?'

'Can't say,' she sighed, pushing hair away from her
face. 'Don't live here. Come over from Medbourne.'
And then, as if remembering, 'Mrs Glassett will be back
– this afternoon. She'll be able to help.'

'Yeah,' he said. 'Probably. Thanks.'

They went out into the sunlight. A breeze pushing
litter in semi-circles by the bus stop. Some kids on
skateboards in the lane by the church.

'What do you think?' he said. 'Where to now?'

She shrugged. 'Brown Street? There are some old people down there.'

They took the first turning past the village store and worked their way down one side and back up the other. Where people weren't out or too young, they either hadn't been living in the village in 1968 or had no memory of an explosion.

'Sure you've got the right place?' said one old man.

Same story in Haydock's Rise and Bessemer Close.

Forty minutes later, they were sitting back on the church wall.

'Someone must have seen or heard something,' Greg said. 'Village full of soldiers – like your grandfather said. Would have stuck in someone's memory.'

'Yeah,' said Inderjit. 'There's some old people in Long Street. That's the road from Stanton. We could knock on a few doors.'

They left his bike and took the hill out of the village. The row of terraces on the near-side; woodland opposite.

'Start at the top?' he said. 'Work our way down?'

There was no answer from the first two houses. They could hear a dog barking in a back room in the second and a harassed woman pulled back the third door. She listened impatiently to the enquiry, and said, 'Look, I'm on the phone. Can you kids call later?' and went back to her conversation.

Ten minutes of this and they were at the bottom of the hill; a string of no answers and 'not interested's stacked up behind.

Number 77 had a chipped blue door and a free paper stuffed in the letter box.

'Yeah?' said a young kid, when they knocked; the sound of a TV cartoon filling the morning. Couldn't be any more than ten, Greg thought.

'Your mum in?' he said. And then: 'Doing a survey.'

The kid turned, shouted down the dark corridor: 'Mum! Someone for you.'

'Who is it?' they heard from a back room. 'What do they want?'

'Jus' a sec,' the kid said and went into the gloom.

Further on down the street a door opened. The white-haired guy that Greg had seen the day before came and stood on the doorstep; looked to where they waited; squinting in the sunlight.

'Yes?' said a middle-aged woman with permed hair and a red face. 'In a bit of a hurry. What do you want?' Looking at each of them.

Out of the corner of his eye, Greg knew that the white-haired guy was still there – looking; listening to the conversation.

Inderjit said quietly: 'Sorry to bother you. We're doing a survey. We need to talk to people who were living in the village in 1968.'

The woman laughed. 'I was here, love, but I was seven in '68. You need to talk to Mrs King.' She nodded towards the end house. 'She was born here. She'll help you.' She draped the teatowel over a radiator. 'She's definitely in because I saw her hanging washing out ten minutes ago. But she's a bit mutt and jeff – you know –' and turned to shout down the corridor. 'Steve – Steve – just going to talk to Avril – won't be a minute.'

She stepped on to the pavement, and walked to the end door, her slippered feet scuffing the pavement. Inderjit followed, and then Greg, who turned and saluted the white-haired guy, a smile touching his lips.

'I'm Celia Jones – I'll just give her a knock. Have to be patient. She's an old lady. In her eighties.'

A couple of cars went past, heading into the village, and they could hear the sound of horses over in the wood beyond the fence. Eventually, there was the shuffling of footsteps approaching from behind the faded green door. It opened after some fumbling, to reveal a grey-haired woman, canted over on a walking stick.

'Sorry to bother you, Avril,' said Mrs Jones, leaning towards her neighbour, 'but these young people want to ask you a few questions. About the sixties.'

'Yes?' said Avril King, peering up at them through lenses dusted with powder. 'I wasn't one of them – you know – hippoes –' a smile pulling the folds of loose flesh on her face.

Celia Jones laughed. 'Hippies,' she said. 'I don't think they're interested in that – are you?' she said, and turned to smile at Inderjit and Greg.

'We're interested in 1968, Mrs King. And what happened round here then,' Greg said.

'That's a long time ago,' she said. 'I was with Harry then, God bless him.'

'Wouldn't keep you long, Mrs King,' said Greg. 'Few questions.' And then: 'It's for work – at school.'

'Look, I'll leave you to sort this out,' Celia Jones said. 'I've got to get to Northampton by one and I'm late. All right?'

'OK,' said Mrs King. 'I'll see you on Friday? As usual?'

'Yes, I'll be round. Got my cousin's pictures of the Rockies,' she said, and turned back to her own door.

'Well, if you're not going to rob me, you might as well come in,' said Avril King. 'Everything's a bit of a mess, but you're very welcome.'

They sat next to each other on a red velvet settee. Soft light coming through net curtains and the smell of dried flowers filling the air.

Avril King sat in her chair, next to an unlit coal fire. The chair seemed to swallow her bent form and she looked up at them with friendly curiosity.

'You hear so many terrible things. About people entering houses and stealing things,' she said. 'But if Celia thinks you're OK, then I won't worry. What is it you wanted to know?'

'We're interested in what happened in November 1968,' said Inderjit. 'Apparently, an RAF aircraft crashed near here, one night. Do you remember that?'

For a moment he thought she hadn't heard or hadn't understood the question. She stared at them, unmoving, and then waved her stick to a couple in a gilt-framed picture, resting on the mantelpiece. 'That's Harry and me. In Weston-super-mare. On our honeymoon. April 1947. He was a fireman. Worked all his life at Market Harborough.'

'Oh, really?' said Greg. 'It's just—'

'That night – I'm not supposed to talk about it. Harry had to sign the Official Secrets Act. Not supposed to breathe a word, about anything. But – well, what I know –'

He didn't hear the rest. Weeks later he remembered

that moment. The instant where the figures on the spreadsheet connected to a dark night in a winter long ago. Whatever had happened was so important everyone involved had been sworn to secrecy. Everything had been hidden, hushed up. He looked at Inderjit, his fingers touching her arm. A slight smile.

Mrs King had stopped talking; was looking at them intently. She said: 'You don't look like spies to me.'

'No,' said Inderjit. 'We're just doing some work, for school. Do you remember that night, Mrs King?'

She leaned back in her chair and closed her eyes. 'Yes,' she said, as if reliving the moment. 'Course I do.' She looked across at them. 'Would you like something to drink? Tea or orange squash? I have some lemonade in the fridge.'

'No, thanks, Mrs King,' Greg said. 'We're fine.'

'Well, that night in November. There was a heck of a storm and we were just going to bed. The phone rang from the station in Harborough. They wanted Harry to get over and help man the reserve engine, because a plane had gone down Creighton Wood way.'

She paused, and adjusted her glasses. Looked again at the photograph on the mantelpiece.

'He was gone. Four or five hours. Not much of a blaze, I don't think, but when he came back he was wearing overalls. They'd taken all his clothes at the crash site; made him shower down and everything.

'He cycled back a day or so later and couldn't get near the place. Soldiers and what-not guarding the wreckage.' She took a deep breath, looked at them both, lines of anger pulling at her face: 'He died of lung cancer. Twelve years ago.' Waited for the words to register, said: 'He never smoked in his life.'

In his head he was back in the library at school. Inderjit sitting before a computer, looking up at him: 'There's something out there that's making these people sick,' she said.

And now she was leaning forward, touching Avril King's arm. She said gently: 'Did he say anything else?'

'No, no. I think he wanted to. We never had secrets from one another.' She sighed. 'There's a cardboard box of his stuff – out in the shed. You can have a look at that, but I don't think you'll find anything. A few photographs; old football medals – that kind of thing.'

She led the way through the kitchen; her stick advancing half a metre at a time, like a climber plunging the stem of an ice-axe into frozen snow.

The back door was open and she pointed to the shed at the end of the small garden, beyond an apple

127

tree. 'Door's on the latch. You'll find the box on the shelf – above the lawnmower.'

'Thanks, Mrs King,' Greg said.

I wasn't expecting anything exciting. Just a pile of souvenirs that marked some old guy's greatest hits. The kind you'd have lying around in a drawer. Small stuff.

It was quite like that. The shed had that tarry smell of creosote and there were loads of cobwebs, dead flies, tins of paint. The cardboard box was exactly where Mrs K said we'd find it – on a shelf next to a can of paraffin.

We took it outside and sat on the lawn – pulling the collection out, bit by bit. From memory, there was stuff like picture postcards and a few old coins. There was also a small wooden box in the corner. Numbers scratched on the lid. Quite heavy – locked.

I was looking around for the key, poking through the medal ribbons and documents, when there was some noise from inside the house. I was looking across at Inderjit when we heard Mrs King say: 'Who called the police?'

Twenty-four

It was more sixth sense than anything, but Greg took the wooden box and threw it over the fence – into the scrubby woodland that bordered the garden. It was swallowed by the ivy ground-cover.

The next moment a couple of police officers barged their way into the garden: all body armour and bulging belts.

Greg and Inderjit had stood up, had left the cardboard box and the stuff scattered on the lawn.

The first policeman, a tall guy carrying a surplus fifty pounds, said: 'We've had a complaint. About you two. Seems you've been knocking on people's doors – making a nuisance of yourselves.'

Behind, they could see Mrs King looking out of the back door, her right hand holding the frame.

The copper had dark hair. He spoke with an urgency that spelt trouble.

'No—' said Greg.

'It seems you tried to con your way into a gentleman's house – just down the road. Yesterday. Now we find you've been doing it here. So, what's all this about – eh?' And he pointed to the box and litter of stuff.

Inderjit said quietly: 'Mrs King said we should have a look.'

The second guy, fair-haired and softly spoken, said: 'Better come wi' us. See if we can sor tit out.'

'Yeah,' said his pal. 'After you've emptied your pockets.' And he indicated that they should dump their stuff on the lawn while he stood and watched, one hand holding his belt.

And when the pathetic collection of tissues and chewing gum and change and phones was spread out; when Greg had tipped his bag on to the grass, the big guy said: 'Right. Put that away and come with us. To the car.'

'Why don't you ask Mrs King?' said Inderjit quietly. 'She'll tell you what we're doing.'

'Sorry, loove, but what you told Mrs King's neither here nor there. We've received a complaint – from a gentleman up the street – and we've got to investigate it.'

As they went through the kitchen, Inderjit leaned towards the old woman and said: 'Don't worry, we'll get this sorted out. We were only trying to find out.'

'I know that, dear,' she said. 'I know what you wanted.'

The car was parked on the left. The white-haired guy stood at his door as they walked past, anger screwed into his face. Inderjit stared at the road, lost to the world.

'So, then,' said the big guy, when he'd closed the driver's door. 'Before we take you to Scotton and book you for conspiracy to defraud members of the public, what have you got to say for yourselves?'

Greg looked out of the window. Saw Mrs Jones's kid, Steve, walk past, staring across at them.

Inderjit said calmly: 'We're doing research for school. We're at Garfield Community College and we have a maths project we're working on. Trying to find out—'

'Just a second,' said the fair-haired copper. 'I need to jot this down,' and he flipped open his notebook. 'Let's have the usual – names, addresses – phone numbers.'

And when that was done, he added, 'So, you're doing some maths project, for school?'

'Yes, that's right,' Inderjit said. 'We've got figures about illness in the area and we're trying to find out why it's so high in this part of the county.'

The big guy leaned back, looked at her. 'So that explains why you're going through the belongings of the old dear at eighty-five, does it? Researching "illness" for school?'

'No – really!' said Greg.

'Now, now – caaalm down,' said the fair-haired guy. 'We take you back to the station and we'll have your parents in and everything. Let's see what we can do, sitting here. Let's keep a lid on things. Awright?'

'Fine with me,' said Greg. And looked out at the street.

Inderjit said nothing; stared at the seat in front of her; chewed her lower lip. When she raised her head, she said: 'We found out – about an aircraft. It crashed thirty years ago, not far from here.'

The northerner said nothing. Turned round in his seat; listened.

'We think that it might be connected to the rise in sickness. From 1968. Mrs King's husband – he was a fireman. Helped put out the fire on the crash site.' She shrugged. 'We were looking at the box of stuff he left behind.'

'You expect us to believe that gibberish,' said the driver, staring ahead; looking up the hill.

'It's the truth,' said Greg, suddenly angry. 'We haven't done anything wrong. There's nothing you can pin on us.'

'We can pin what we like. On the pair of you,' said the copper, looking back. 'And what we say'll make a lot more sense than this – garbage.'

'Why do you think a plane crash might have led to – sickness breaking out?' the other said. 'I don't see the connection mesel.'

'Not the only one,' said his mate.

'We don't know either. That's the only thing we can find. We're trying to make the connection,' Inderjit said. 'Trying to link one with the other.'

And that was that. Another couple of minutes and the fair-haired guy – the northerner – said: 'You can't just go into people's houses like that. Not nowadays. Old people get nervous. They read about break-ins and violence. The gentleman who called us was really bothered. Thought Mrs King was at risk. If you want to do something like this, you're going to need a letter. From your headteacher.'

'OK,' said Inderjit. 'I see.'

'So, what my colleague is saying,' said the burly driver, turning round in his seat, 'we don't want our time wasted on some kind of wild goose chase. Bang on another door today and we'll be back – and we'll book you.'

And so they were let off and let out.

They trudged back up the hill in silence. The police car crawling past, coppers staring straight ahead.

'I'll get the box,' Greg said to Inderjit, as he turned the key in the bike lock. 'Take it home. Have a look. Send you an email.'

'Be careful,' she said, her hand touching his arm. 'Wouldn't want you to get into any more – you know – trouble.'

'I know,' he said. 'Thanks.'

As he pedalled away, he wondered what kind of report the policemen would make. Wondered whether someone like Bonnington would get to hear of the incident. That guy in the four-by-four with the soft voice and police radio, who knew his mother.

For the first time Greg began to feel uneasy about the investigation. Tried to imagine where it was headed; what secret the wooden box contained.

What had Harry King seen that needed the Official Secrets Act to gag his mouth?

Twenty-five

The old guy wasn't around when Greg freewheeled past; Inderjit standing at the top of the hill watching him go. A light touch on the left hand, easing back the brake. Didn't stop immediately after Mrs King's house; waited for the bend to provide cover, before dismounting.

He hauled his bike up the low bank, through the scattering of trees and over the spread ivy. Left his wheels behind as he approached the side of the house.

There was no one in the garden: the box of stuff, the contents they'd scattered over the lawn, had been put away; the shed door shut. He waited; allowed the silence to settle. Watched the patch of land ahead to see whether Mrs King was around. No one in the garden beyond either. Birds silent overhead, as though everyone was waiting for him to make his move.

He didn't find the box straight away. There were too many trees; too much ground cover to simply drop his hands into the green and find it. He moved slowly, watching the garden, always ready to freeze in case the back door opened and the old lady stepped out. Listened for the crack of twigs beneath his feet; the air heavy with dead vegetation. Wondered what had happened to the police car.

He felt the box as he trod through the ivy. Like finding an unexpected step, a discarded brick. In slow motion, he bent down and pulled it clear; all the time, listening for footfalls behind, the creak of a door ahead.

And then it was in his hands – heavier than he remembered and with the numbers scratched on the surface. Like a message.

Within two minutes, he was standing back on the pavement, the box stowed and the Ordnance Survey map spread over the handlebars; his eyes scanning the trails and roads to see whether the footpath that went through Creighton Wood and bypassed the wasteland beyond, wound in the direction of Gretford.

Have another look at the small patch of wilderness, he thought.

But the footpath trailed north and then north-west, before losing itself in a side road south of Clipston. He grunted and folded the stiff paper; slung his leg over the crossbar and pushed down the slope towards Stanton.

The thing about the box was that it was as heavy as a brick. Carefully made from some pale wood, the joints dovetailed, and the lock edged with brass. When you shook it, there was no sound: it was solid; packed tight.

If Harry King had locked it, then it must contain something he wanted to keep safe.

Then there was the thing about the numbers. Why would anyone roughly scratch six digits into the top of the box? The numbers shouted out; drew attention to themselves. They'd been made with something like a nail, gouging a couple of millimetres into the surface.

Could be a phone number, he thought, turning the sequence over; trying the different combinations:

705756.

705 756.

70 57 56.

The number of a key, maybe? Perhaps they connected to the contents of the box, in some way? Get inside and the numbers might make sense.

He picked up some gum at a shop in Stanton and then settled in to the climb along the side of the hill before the drop into the valley. Resumed thinking about the numbers. Turned over the sequence. Tried to pull them into sense. Remembered the last time he'd been this way, he'd met that guy Bonnington. The man with the soft voice. Who knew his mother. What was that all about?

Up ahead there was a vehicle just tucked into the passing-place at the side of the road: a dark green four-by-four, its left indicator blinking in the spread of shadows. The outline of a single driver, canted over to the right; looking in the side mirror.

And behind? He heard the sound of the six-cylinder Ford when he was no more than fifty metres from the off-road. The revs kept low as the car stayed at his pace; the purr of the tyres like a threat.

He knew what he would see even as he turned his head to check: knew the two occupants; saw the polished white and two-tone gantry of the squad car.

Twenty-six

Perhaps it was because of all the cycling, the trudging up and down streets, the interview with the coppers – but I suddenly knew what was going to happen. Seen the film, got the T-shirt etcetera etcetera. I'd get level with the rear door and the front would suddenly swing open and I'd be pitched into the road, coppers in the car waiting while that guy Bonnington pushed the gear stick forward and eased away – disappearing round the bend while I wiped blood off my face.

I didn't hang around for that. Didn't wait for the ambush but pulled over behind the car, planted a foot on the ground and lifted my mobile from my shirt pocket. Like I was calling for help.

But the squad car carried on down the hill, the thin face of the northern copper looking out.

Another face looked at me from the back of the four-by-four: long and narrow, with the bright eyes of a German Shepherd. There was a woman at the wheel, talking into a phone and studying me in the rear-view. Checking to see why the dog was suddenly restless.

The car didn't move and Greg replaced his phone, pushed out on to the road; didn't look back as he picked up the steady, cross-country rhythm.

He felt stupid at his sudden fear, at his panic. 'What a joke,' he said aloud, and spat into the road. Like a scene out of a bad film.

Just short of Gretford, he stopped at the entrance to a field and dropped his bike by a gate; unhitched his bag. He sat on the top bar and pulled out the box; felt the dull weight of it fill his hands; ran his fingers over the scratched numbers. Tried to prise the lid using thumb and forefinger, but it was secure.

In his bag, he found the old tobacco tin, with the puncture repair kit and the wooden-handled clasp knife. He jammed the tip of the blade between the lid and the box, just short of the lock; dug it in and levered up, feeling the blade flex, and then, with a sudden rupture that almost unbalanced him, the top sprang back and he was looking down into a square of black plastic — folded over and fixed with tape. A label read: 705756.

He pulled out the package, dropped the box and cut through the tape. Just dry, powdery earth. Maybe half a kilo, something like that. No gold dust or platinum, just common or garden dirt. He held a handful in his palm.

It was like at every turn the mystery got deeper; the more clues you got, the further you were pulled in, the more you didn't know, couldn't figure out.

He jumped down and stuffed the package into the container and pulled out his mobile. Called up a fresh SMS: '*Box full of earth,*' he texted. Scrolled Inderjit's number and sent it into the ether.

His mobile rang as he took the bridge over the A14; four lanes of traffic forty feet down.

'Yeah,' he said, cupping the phone.

'What kind of earth?' she said.

Even through the rush of cars he could hear the ring of her bangles.

'Just dirt. Nothing else.'

'In a packet?'

'Yeah – sealed with tape. The number on the box scribbled on a label – 705756.'

'One second,' she said, and he could hear her searching for a pen. 'OK. I'll have a think. Will text you later.'

'How's your grandfather?' he said.

'He's got oxygen – he may be going away tomorrow,' she said. He saw her bent over the phone, leaning

141

into the chat; grandmother sitting in the yellow light watching that tired face.

'Sorry.'

'Lived with it. For months,' she said. 'He's had good care. We have no complaints.' She sounded like her mother.

He heard a loud call from inside the house – 'Inderjit?' – and she said, 'I have to go now. Be careful.'

And she was gone, her voice whipped away, and he was left watching the cars stream below.

Twenty-seven

He got back to the house a shade after two. There was no car outside and no note on the kitchen table. He went up to his room, emptied his bag and crashed out on the bed. Wondered about the box — and the plastic bag — stuffed away in his sock drawer; turned over the brush with the police.

He woke to the sound of the key in the door.

'Hi!' his mother called. 'I'm back.'

Twenty past three.

When he reached the kitchen, she was bent over the table, reading an obituary in the paper — some legendary pop star who'd taken leave of the planet.

'D'you want some tea?' he said, lifting the kettle.

'Yes. Please.' And then: 'What have you been up to?'

'Oh, this and that,' he said, flipping the switch. 'Noodles and stir-fry later?'

She didn't say anything, but he knew she'd stopped reading.

'There's some vegetables in the fridge that'll go off,' he said.

'I had to call back this morning,' she said. 'Left some stuff in the front room.'

'Yeah – and?' he said.

'Don't "Yeah – and" me like that,' she said. 'You know jolly well that you should have been here. You know what your father said. I feel really let down, Greg. This is dishonest. After everything you promised.'

She was standing up, holding the chair back with her left hand. Watching as he lifted a carton of milk from the fridge.

'So,' she said. 'Where were you?'

He dropped tea bags into the pot, said: 'If I told you, you wouldn't believe me.'

Not the answer she was expecting. He could tell by the silence; felt her looking at him. Surprised. 'Go on,' she said.

He looked across at her. Wondered for a moment, and then changed his mind. 'I went down the library. Again. I know I should have told you about it. Sorry.'

She shrugged and looked down at the paper. 'Your father will be phoning tonight. You better have a word. Tell him what you've been up to.' She went out into the hall.

'Yeah,' he said. 'Thanks.' And then, calling after her:

'That guy, Bonnington – the guy in the picture. Who was he?'

When she came back, she said: 'Why do you ask?'

'Just wondered, that's all. A coincidence – seeing him and the photograph and—'

'Have you seen him again?'

He fetched mugs from the cupboard. 'No – I haven't seen him again.'

She pulled her diary from her bag; flipped through some pages and made a note. 'He had some government job,' she said. 'Civil servant. Something like that.'

He looked over the garden; at the starlings on the lawn. The leaves of the poinsettia on the window ledge were starting to hang down. He stuffed his finger in the pot: earth like dust. Checked the instructions on the card: soil conditions, moisture, temperature, sunlight.

Soil conditions.

What the soil consisted of. The mineral content. Earth varied from place to place. The stuff in the back garden wasn't the same as the dust in the poinsettia pot. Or the dirt hidden in the box in his sock drawer.

He poured boiling water into the teapot and then went into the hall and pulled the Yellow Pages from the shelf.

S for Soil.

S for – Soil Analyst

'*Need to make the best of YOUR garden or small-holding?*' he read. '*Then you need to know your soil. Laboratory-performed analysis will provide you with a pH reading and breakdown of mineral and organic content. Call Middle Earth today*'.

Yeah, he thought. Why not? And wrote the number on a scrap torn from the shopping list by the breadbin.

'Going to check emails,' he said and walked past his mother, who was scanning the letters page. She didn't answer.

'Middle Earth — soil analyst?' he said.

'Can I help you?'

'I've got some soil — could you have a look at it for me?' he said.

There was silence at the other end. In the background, Greg could hear the whine of an electric guitar: some axeman bending the notes, face distorted.

'You mean, you've got a garden you'd like us to look at?' the guy said.

'Nope. Just a packet of soil. I want to know what's in it.'

'O-Kay,' he said, stretching the word. 'Aw right. Come over when you like and we'll have a look.'

'How do I find you?' said Greg. 'I'm on my bike.'

'No problemo,' the guy said. 'You know the jitty on

146

Southfield Avenue? Just past the allotments? The cut-through to the industrial estate? Yeah? We're there. On the corner. Middle Earth.'

'See you later,' Greg said.

A text message had arrived whilst he'd been talking. It was from Inderjit. Four words. One kiss.

'*Numbs r map ref.*'

Twenty-eight

Ten to four. That was the frigging time, he told Raff later. When the text came through and the pieces started to drop into place; the dots got to be joined up.

He pressed the call button: dialled Inderjit. Listened to the phone turn over. Just the voice mail.

'Thanks,' he said. 'Got the text. You've some brain, to spot that. Talk later.' He paused, watched a couple of skateboarders across the road. 'Hope your grandfather is OK. Thinking of you.' Snapped the off button.

Of course it was a six-figure map reference. The earth had come from the location scratched on the box. A marker to the past. Could have shone a ten-metre neon sign and he'd still have missed it.

He went over to his bag and hauled out the map; spread it across the table.

705756. .

Connect the eastings with the northings – join

together longitude and latitude – and hey presto – accurate to a hundred metres, less.

70 on the longitude scale took you over to the west of the map. And 75? The two lines crossed south of the stream and footpath – just beyond Creighton Wood. Close to where Bonnington had rolled up; said to back off.

Where the bomber had crashed those years ago.

The kids outside had moved away. A young woman with a pushchair went past. She was bent over, talking to her child, smiling.

The earth was connected to the Canberra bomber. It was taken from near the crash site. Grabbed by a fireman named Harry King those years before.

Harry King had been silenced by the law – made to sign the Official Secrets Act – but he must have seen something – or found out something. He couldn't talk about it – but he decided to keep the earth – like a sample – and signpost it by carving the OS map reference on the lid.

Is that what happened?

He went downstairs, to where his mother was sipping tea and writing on the shopping list. He said: 'I'd like to call in at the library? Just to check if they've got this book – on statistics?'

She placed her mug on the table, pushed a strand of hair from her face, said: 'Won't it wait?'

He shrugged: 'Maybe – but I was hoping to get this sorted. Before Suli comes around. Tomorrow night.' The impossible offer; the loaded dice.

She sighed: 'OK. Thirty minutes, Greg.' Eyes narrowed; as if she meant it.

'Sure,' he said. 'No problem.'

Middle Earth was on Southfield Avenue, a couple of hundred metres from the railway embankment. Greg circled the roundabout at the junction and cruised on to the pavement. A shopfront full of plants and adverts for organic stuff. A couple of compost bins; tubs containing great trumpets of colour.

Inside? A dry smell of old earth and fresh vegetation; racks of seeds and shelves sorted with packets and bottles.

Straight ahead a white guy with shoulder-length hair and a wispy beard reading a book on Patagonia.

'Hi,' said Greg, walking over. 'Called a few minutes ago? About the soil sample?'

'Right,' the guy said, placing the book on the counter. 'Got the stuff?'

Greg reached into the bag and pulled out the packet; passed it across.

'OK,' he said, 'Let's see,' and grabbed a handful of dirt; rubbed the soil between thumb and forefinger. 'Feels like clay,' he said. 'Not a lot of organic content. Pretty heavy to cultivate.' He looked up. 'Drains badly, you see. Hard work overall. You want me to check the pH, organic and mineral content? The works?'

'Yeah,' Greg said. 'It's just – the soil doesn't come from round here. Not from the garden or anything.'

'Yeah?' said the guy, stroking the hair on his chin. 'Take a seat,' motioning Greg to the chair by the counter. 'Robin Young –' extending a dusty hand. 'Want some tea?'

'No – you're all right,' Greg said, leaning back, looking round. 'The soil probably comes from farmland. About fifteen miles away.'

'Right,' Young said, nodding, 'right.'

'It's been wrapped up. Shoved away – for thirty years. Maybe more.'

Robin Young leaned on his elbows; chin resting on his hands. Through the unbuttoned shirt Greg saw a *CND* badge hanging from his neck. Campaign for Nuclear Disarmament, Greg thought. Has to be on my side of the wire.

'OK,' he said, sitting up. 'I don't know anything about soil or plants or anything – but – about thirty years ago, an RAF aircraft crashed on some land this side of

Stanton. The soil comes from the crash site; picked up by a fireman.'

They listened to the whine of a train on the embankment.

'Right,' Robin Young said. 'So, so you're not intending to grow anything with it?'

'No,' Greg said, and laughed for the first time in about a year. 'Just need to know what's in it.'

'Any ideas?' Young said. 'Any guesses?'

'You tell me,' Greg said.

'Do – ah – do you think the plane crash may have affected the soil in some way?'

Greg shrugged. 'Don't know,' he said. 'But – I think it's possible. Yeah,' thinking of Harry King. 'Pretty likely, I would say. How much do I owe you?'

'Ordinarily? Twenty-five pounds – but we'll see when you come back.' Handing over a Middle Earth business card.

'When can you tell me what you've found?' Greg said, bending down to snap the catches on his bag.

'Not much on at the moment. Tomorrow lunchtime?'

'Yeah,' Greg said. 'I'll be back.'

As he turned to go, Young said: 'Anybody know – about this? Anybody know you've got it?'

'Just my partner,' Greg said. 'And you.'

Twenty-nine

'Your mother said you were missing today.' His father speaking from a hotel room. His voice like a kitchen knife. Greg imagined him sitting in the twilight; a square of paper placed at right-angles; fingers strangling the receiver.

'Library,' Greg said. 'Stats stuff. For this maths project.'

Greg listened to the silence; his mother in the lounge; TV turned low.

'You didn't ask – p-p-p-permission,' his father said.

'Slipped up there,' Greg said. And then: 'I have apologised.'

'Makes no – not a jot – of difference,' his father said. 'You know the rules. You want to go out – even into the g-g-garden – you ask.' Silence. 'Got that?'

'OK,' Greg said. 'I understand your concern.'

'And d-d-don't be sarcastic.'

'Talk to you later,' Greg said, suddenly feeling torn up. Like discussing the time of day with the speaking clock. Today's instructions have been brought to you by *Strange, Stuttering Dad*.

Hand covering the receiver, Greg called out: 'Do you want to speak to Dad?'

Later, his mother came into the kitchen where Greg was applying a knife to a pepper: turning it into a pile of red strips.

'He's just thinking – of your own best interests,' she said. 'You know that, don't you?' Looking into the side of his face.

'He has a great way of putting it.'

He pulled celery from its plastic, reached for the vegetable brush.

'He doesn't want you – to get into trouble. He thinks – what with the Carl business –'

'What – that I'm off my head –?' He turned, kitchen knife gripped in his hand. 'That I might kill someone?'

She went over to the table; folded the pages of the newspaper.

'Stuff happened, Greg—'

He could hear the rush of a train. On the wall, a poppy field print. On the stairs, the picture of Sarah.

'You can't pin that on me. I didn't kill my sister,' he said, placing the knife carefully on the chopping board.

She looked down at the table; at the spread of news. Eyes filling up.

Suli phoned at six. Said, 'How're you doing? Going to that party – on Saturday – at Catherine Baker's?'

He leaned against the door frame. Closed his eyes. Thought about Fraser. That was so – something else. 'Yeah,' he said at last. 'You?'

'Not invited – me and Dilshad going to see "Highway" – if you change your mind –'

'Thanks,' he said. 'Sounds good. I'll call you. Tomorrow. I'll have to go – sorting tea.'

One of those moments, those memories, he thought about, days later, when he was miles away and sleeping under a strange roof. Hearing again Suli's chatter. A lifetime away, even then.

The radio excused their conversation that last night. Some quiz show with ex-public schoolboys – a half hour of wordplay and double meanings. Applause echoing in some dusty old studio.

'I'm meeting your father in Northampton. Tomorrow night,' she said. 'Off the train. Going to have a meal in Sorentino's.' She looked across at him. 'Do you want to come?'

Nah, he thought. Rather stick pins in my eyes. 'No

thanks,' he said shortly. 'Bit too soon for kiss and make up. Don't you think?'

'Whatever,' she said, pushing her plate to one side. 'Your funeral.'

'Yeah,' he said. 'Thanks for the thought,' and headed for the sink.

James Dean looked morose when Greg reached his room. Like a half tonne of broken rock had landed on his shoulders. 'You and me both,' Greg said, and slumped in his chair.

He leaned forward and switched on the computer. What he really should do was talk to his parents, get their view on the situation.

He leaned back and smiled. He couldn't imagine any situation where the three of them could ever get together for some cosy fireside chat. To sort things out. His father would simply bang on about 'irresponsibility' and 'breaking the rules' – and his mother? She'd just sit there, looking sorrowful.

He thought back to the meeting with Bonnington – the strange see-saw of his voice. His mother said that he was some kind of civil servant, but what did that mean? He remembered the radio in the car, the request for an update. Bonnington was some kind of policeman. But what could you police on the site of an old aircraft crash? And what did his mother really know about him? He remembered her unease when he'd looked at the photographs, asked the question. What was that all about?

The internet icon flashed a new arrival.

Got your message. Sorry I didn't reply. Ambulance took Nannaji away this p.m. The doctor says he might not survive the night. The nurses are very good, but Nanniji is upset.

   I'm here all evening.

   Inderjit x

Message sent at 6.10. Forty minutes ago.

He imagined her sitting at the computer, dark hair draped over her shoulders; mother in the corner, staring at the television. Alert for the phone. The tack-tack of nails on plastic, as Inderjit touched the keys. Reaching up with her right hand to push back her hair.

'What are you doing?' her mother would say.

'Sending an email.'

'Not to that English boy? The *gora*? You mustn't encourage him. Let him stick with his own.'

'He's just a friend, Mum,' she'd say, adding another line. 'Someone I work with. On my Maths GCSE.'

'Some friend who spends his days cycling half way

across the county. Just to see you. Why couldn't he use the phone?'

But then, maybe it wouldn't be like that. Maybe Inderjit's mother would go to her room and Inderjit would simply stare into the TV screen, waiting for the call from the hospice. Squashed into the corner of an armchair, legs drawn up.

He pulled a fresh page on to the screen. Rubbed his eyes; hit the keys.

Hi Inderjit, he wrote, *Hope everything isn't too bad.*

Sorry to hear about your grandfather. I know you were expecting him to go to the hospice, but it must have come as a shock. The nurses will be good to him and your grandmother.

I took the earth down to this place in town. The guy there said he'd tell me about it tomorrow. It might be interesting – might contain nothing. I'll let you know.

Look after yourself.

Greg x

He leaned back in his chair, wondered again about Bonnington and the cops. Wondered what they were up to.

Outside there was a loud blast from someone's horn; the sound of rubber pulling from a floored pedal. He got up and looked out. Red tail lights glowing at the roundabout. A couple turning to stare. A dark saloon on the far side, two hundred metres down, parked in front of a street light. Someone behind the wheel; thrown into shadow.

When he looked again, an hour later, the car was still there and the guy hadn't moved.

Thirty

'*What did you do at nursery today? Did you have a good time?*'

'*Yes.*'

'*What sort of things did you do?*'

'*We did painting and – and – sticking.*'

'*Painting and sticking? Did you paint a picture? What did you paint?*'

'*Mummy and Geg. At the seaside.*'

'*Were they making sandcastles?*'

'*Geg had a spade. A big spade. There was a – a seagull. We fed the seagull.*'

He woke hearing Sarah's voice. Months left to live, she spoke in the dark about their last holiday, at Weymouth. He remembered his father in the lounge with the tape running and Sarah on the sofa, her doll in her lap.

Someone had placed the old tape in the cassette

player of his stereo. Her voice, eight years dead, speaking to him in the two o'clock dark.

He snapped the light switch; leaned over and stopped the cassette. Stopped the voice. But there was something else; another sound in the room; the slow shuffle of rollers pulling paper through the printer. The operating light blinking on the far side; the movement of the print head sending its own Morse.

He rubbed his face and sat on the side of the bed; wondered what else the night had to deliver.

Out on the street, the black saloon had gone. Further down, on the left, another car, outside the Bandaranaikas'. The glow of a cigarette in the driver's seat. Everything dark.

He lifted the first sheet from the tray; carried it to the bed. Stretched back and leaned against the headboard. Avoided the stare of James Dean.

Mummy was outside, he read. *I was playing in my room, with my soldiers. They were in a war and I'd used bricks to build a fort. Sarah was playing on the landing. I could hear her singing. Sometimes she talked to herself. She had her dolls spread out and they were talking in different voices.*

She came into my room and sat on my skateboard. She said: 'What you doing?' and I told her about the war and the soldiers. She said, 'Can I play? Can I play with the soldiers, Geg?'

I said that she couldn't. I didn't think she'd understand about war or anything. She was rocking backwards and forwards on the board. She said: 'Can I take my dolls for a ride on your skateboard?'

I thought that was all right and I said that she could. And so she pushed it out of the door.

I could hear the wheels of the skateboard on the carpet, and Sarah laughing. I thought she was pushing her dolls backwards and forwards. Giving them a ride, like she'd said.

The noise got faster and faster and then there was a cry. I think she called 'Geg' and then there was a crash. She fell down the stairs. Over and over.

He reached the end of the page; went over to the printer and lifted the second sheet.

Sarah was lying at the bottom of the stairs. Her head was turned to the side and her arm was sticking out. There was blood under her head. She didn't move. She didn't make any noise. I ran down the stairs. I said: 'Sarah, wake up.' I thought that she was pretending.

But she didn't wake up and I didn't know what to do. I called for Mum but she wasn't around. I ran into the lounge and the kitchen, shouting for help.

162

When I got back to the hall, Sarah was still lying there. I tried to move her, to lift her up, thinking that might be of some use, but she was too heavy and I could only drag her a little way.

I left her there and went upstairs into my parents' room and looked out. Maybe I was hoping that someone in the street might help, I don't know.

There was a car parked on the other side of the hedge. A grey Ford. There was a couple in the front seats. A man in a black jacket, with dark grey hair, was sitting behind the wheel. He was leaning to his left, his arms around this woman. I couldn't see her face. She had her head on his shoulder. Her eyes were closed. When she looked out, I could see that it was my mother.

Thirty-one

Sarah Price died of a broken neck. That's what they said at the inquest. She died on a Saturday afternoon in October. His father had been away on business and his mother – elsewhere.

The police came to the house. Talked to his parents. Greg sat in the lounge and listened to a woman in a black sweater ask questions for the best part of an hour. Sitting on the sofa with the holiday picture of Weymouth staring back. He didn't say a word. Kept his seven-year-old trap shut.

He never spoke about Sarah's death. Never opened his mouth about his mother. Never answered when the woman in the dark sweater said: 'Did you have an argument with your sister, Greg?'

'Death by misadventure,' that's what the coroner said. Sarah had died as a result of an accident. She'd been playing and had fallen down the stairs.

Each September they went over to the grave, on her

birthday, and placed some flowers in the jar; stood around feeling awkward. Wondered where she was, what she might be thinking.

For weeks, months, Greg was convinced that he'd come home and Sarah would be there, running down the hall with some new story from nursery.

It never happened. But Sarah never slipped away. Her photograph was a daily reminder of who she'd once been, and her memory filled the spaces between them with blame. They all remembered that her body had been found at the foot of the stairs next to Greg's skateboard.

Eventually, like after fifteen minutes, Greg got up and switched off the computer and printer; placed the cassette back into its box; folded the sheets of A4 and placed them in his bedside drawer.

He lay in bed and turned over the past and everything that was crowding the present. Later, when he told Raff about the incident − of the cassette and the printout − Raff just touched his arm and said, 'Stuff happens.' And then: 'Something you set up in your sleep?'

Greg shrugged. 'I guess,' he said.

When he thought about it, he realised that the whole episode of Sarah's death was something he'd filed away in the drawer marked 'Later'. Waiting for some special moment where he could talk about what really happened – how he couldn't say about his mother because she was sitting with her head drooped over some guy, who wasn't his father, while her daughter lay in a pool of blood from a head fracture.

He lay through the dark hours and wondered what he was going to do.

Outside there was someone pulling on a cigarette and staring into the dark. Who was he? What was that all about? What was he waiting for? Or was it all his imagination that an ambush was waiting round every corner?

He drifted off to sleep, and the next thing was the bleat along the corridor, from his parents' room. The sound of the 7.30 call.

Later, his mother splashing water in the bathroom; the whisk of her toothbrush coming and going as she walked back and forth, turning thoughts whilst polishing her teeth.

She came in just before 8.30, plastered with make-up, and wearing her red jacket and blue jeans. Probably trying to distract attention from the wreck of her face.

'Sleep well?' she said, and went over to wrench back the curtains.

'Not particularly,' he said.

'Thought I heard the printer – in the night,' she said. 'About two-ish?'

'Yeah – it seems to have a mind of its own,' he said. 'Gave me a shock.'

'Well, anyway,' she said. 'I'm sorting out some stuff at school this morning and meeting Briony for lunch.'

'Yeah?' he said, staring down the length of the bed. 'I know about the curfew, so please—'

'How do you feel?'

'Fine.' He looked up at her. 'The shingles has gone.'

'OK,' she said, checking her watch, 'I'd better go. I'll be back about half-two.'

A couple of minutes later, he heard the door slam and then the cough of the engine turning over. It didn't move for a minute and he wondered whether she was having second thoughts about leaving, but eventually there was the scrape into first gear and soon the fading drone as she headed towards the roundabout and the short cut to the estate.

Later, after he'd got dressed, he saw a blue hatchback parked on the near side. The single driver looking down, checking something on his lap.

Maybe there always were people around, sitting in their cars, checking stuff; maybe this was just paranoia –

something he'd noticed because of the meeting with Bonnington. But it didn't feel like that.

Inderjit called at just after ten. He was reading the transfer news and eating cereal in the kitchen when the phone rang.

'Yeah?' he said, his eyes scanning the comments about the Spanish striker Leicester had signed.

'I'm in Gretford,' she said. Her voice muffled. Sounding like she had a cold. The natural rhythm, light and shade, damped down.

'How's it going?' he asked. 'Where are you?'

'Hospice,' she said, and broke off to blow her nose. 'Been here about all night. Passed your house at ten yesterday.'

'How's your grandfather?

'He's – ah – he's –' and she broke off to blow her nose. 'He doesn't have long. We're going to go home to get washed and have a sleep. Be back later. If you're around—'

'Yeah – I could get over,' he said.

'It's hard to say. I'll text you. Maybe late afternoon. How's everything going?'

He tried to imagine her outside the hospice; standing in front of the small lawn and the banked flowers; head bent and phone clamped to her ear, tissue scrunched up in her hand.

'So-so,' he said. 'We're on to something.'

'Tell me – later,' she said. 'I have to go now.'

Maybe she had more sense than he did, he thought later, when he was travelling away from Gretford. More sense about knowing when to be silent. Knowing when to shut up.

Thirty-two

He walked down the road to where the hatchback was parked. Walked with his hands up in idiot surrender; a broad smile attached to his face, as if to say, 'Here I am, let's get it over with!' An old man stopping to stare.

Greg stood looking in at the guy who was talking into some invisible microphone, his lips moving and his eyes hidden behind a set of shades. Cropped dark hair and high cheekbones; T-shirt and jeans. He stopped talking, gestured to the nearside passenger door.

'Take a seat,' he said shortly when Greg looked in. 'Come on, I don't have all day. Just need to have a chat.'

'Yeah?' said Greg. 'Why's that then?' Holding on to the roof of the car.

'At the police station. Won't take long,' the guy said, tossing a clipboard into the back seat. 'Nothing heavy.'

Greg considered. 'Who are you?' he said. 'Been camped outside my house for hours.'

The guy sighed, reached into his jeans' pocket and pulled out a tattered identity card. An old passport photograph on the left. Detective Sergeant Steve Dawson in bold type. County police badge. A scribbled signature.

'Nice picture,' said Greg, 'but what do you want to talk about?'

Dawson looked across: 'Someone wants to have a word. That's all.'

'Why not call in at the house? Why hang around outside all night?'

'Look,' said the policeman. 'We want to talk to you. About an incident – thirty-odd years ago. OK?'

Greg looked down the road. There was a woman just going into the baker's; a girl on a bike heading into town. No one else around.

'OK,' he said, and pulled open the door. 'Am I under arrest?'

'Nothing like that,' said Dawson, turning the key in the ignition. 'Just a chat.'

Greg clipped the seat belt and sat back; watched the ordinary life of Gretford stumble past. He saw a kid from his year over by the computer shop; Mrs Granger with her husband. Wondered who wanted to talk to him.

The car pulled up next to a police van in the small

car park at the back of the station, just up from the parish church.

'Follow me,' the guy said and led the way, in through a metal-framed door, down a corridor to a reception desk. A woman sergeant looking up when they appeared.

She looked behind at Greg and muttered: 'IR2's free – you can use that.' Face a blank. 'Teas and coffees?'

'You want anything to drink?' Dawson said, turning to Greg. 'They've probably got squash or juice.'

'Nah,' said Greg, hands stuffed into his pockets; smile fixed in place.

IR2 was a small, windowless room with four chairs, a table and two microphones. There were no filing cabinets, notices or books. There was no echo. Their footsteps sank into the pile of the carpet. Everything muffled.

'Take a seat,' the guy said, gesturing to a chair. 'I'll get the paperwork and we'll have a chat.'

Greg sat down. He said: 'Thought someone wanted to see me? I thought that was—'

'Later,' Dawson said, by the door. 'You need to be patient.'

When he came back, with a grey folder, Greg said, 'Don't I need a lawyer or something?'

'This isn't a big deal, Greg,' Dawson said. 'We're just having a chat. That's all. A bit later on, there's someone else who wants to talk to you.'

'OK,' Greg shrugged. 'OK.'

Dawson pulled out some sheets of A4. The usual set of references at the top. Dates and times running down the left, keeping pace with the paragraphs. Even upside down Greg could see that his name and address headed the page.

'So, Greg,' began Dawson, looking up at him. 'You visited Hindlip yesterday. Tell me about that.'

He had a direct stare; looked across the table with his eyebrows drawn together. No hint of a smile. Like talking to a Year Head. Same situation; different room.

'Why do you want to know?' Greg said. 'I was just seeing a friend.'

Dawson looked down. 'You visited Inderjit Sandhu, a female student who's recently started at Garfield Community College.'

It wasn't a question: it was a statement of fact.

'You want to go on?' said Greg. 'You seem to know all about it anyway.'

'Why did you go to see Inderjit?'

'Isn't it all written down?' He stretched across and tapped the paper. 'Somewhere down there?'

'Just answer the question,' said Dawson.

Greg leaned back, slouched down. He wondered what James Dean would have said; what advice the silent one could have offered.

'I went to Hindlip – because of some research we've been doing – about sickness in the county. That's it.'

'And?'

'What do you mean?'

'You called in to talk to Mrs Avril King – in Long Street.'

'Yeah – so?'

'And whilst there, you removed an item that belonged to her husband –'

'Oh, yeah, right,' said Greg. 'And the rest. You'll be accusing me of grievous bodily harm next.' He looked round the room; rubbed his eyes.

'Well,' said Dawson. 'Mrs King was taken to Harborough District hospital last night.' He paused; looked across the table; checked Greg's reaction.

Greg sat still for a moment; remembered the old woman half-swallowed by her chair, telling them about the explosion. 'What's happened to her?' he said.

'She was taken ill after it was disclosed that an item belonging to her husband had been removed during your visit.'

'I don't know what you're talking about,' he said.

It was suddenly hard to breathe; like he'd missed his footing – had slipped beneath the surface. He saw the old woman talking quietly about the past; leading them out to the garden. Now this.

Dawson put down the file. Straightened the paper. Looked severe. Like some Deputy Head who was getting impatient. 'We're not here to waste time, Greg. So, tell me: what did you take?'

'How do you know I took anything?' Chin up; defiant. 'Police were there – we were searched. They didn't find – anything.'

'You're a time-waster, you know that, don't you?' said Dawson, reaching into his pocket and pulling out a cassette tape. 'A complete waste of space.' Inserting the cassette into a wall-mount; pressed play.

There was the usual two seconds of hiss as the leader tape took up the slack; bits of static, and then through the whine and fuzz of interference, a conversation:

'*What kind of earth?*'

'*Just dirt. Nothing else.*'

'*In a packet?*'

'*Yeah – sealed with tape. The number on the box scribbled on a label – 705756.*'

Greg sitting astride his bike, on the bridge over the A14. The crematorium ahead and Inderjit's voice in his ear.

Dawson switched the machine off. Looked down at the sheaf of papers, said: 'What kind of earth?'

'Is it legal to do this?' Greg said. 'To listen in to people's conversations?'

'Tell me about the dirt in the packet.'

'What do you want to know?'

'What you've done with it.'

'You brought me here to find out what I've done with dirt from some box? Why didn't you batter the door down – yesterday? Search the house?'

'Where have you put the box, Greg?'

He leaned back and thought of the guy in Middle Earth. Long hair and questions about pH values. Dawson staring across the table with a taped conversation. Mrs King lying sick over in Harborough; Inderjit's grandfather dying a few streets away.

The box was important. That's why Harry King had hidden it. That's why Dawson wanted to get hold of it. The box was valuable.

'Well?' said Dawson. 'I haven't got all day.'

But then, of course, Greg didn't have to answer because the door opened and Bonnington walked in.

Thirty-three

'Thanks,' he said to Dawson. 'I'll take over – if you want to remove the tape.'

He came and sat opposite Greg. Looked down at the page of notes that Dawson had left and reached into an inside pocket for his glasses. Took them off when he looked up, eyes like flint; grey hair cut close; the smudge of sun on his cheeks. Like the memory of some holiday.

'Thank you for coming,' he said. 'I appreciate it must be a bit strange.' Applying a hammer to the vowels.

Greg said nothing.

'Hope this isn't too much of a surprise – after our chat the other afternoon, out in the countryside.' Amusement playing around his eyes, his mouth. 'How's your mother these days?'

Greg shrugged; stared at the table.

'I knew her, you know – vaguely – few years ago,' Bonnington said.

Greg could feel a muscle catch at the corner of his eye. Felt his breath shorten. 'She's – OK,' he said.

'Ye-es,' said Bonnington. 'She was a chipper lass, a few years back.'

'Don't know what you mean.'

'No?' said Bonnington, a glance of concern. 'She was – cut up – about that tragic business – Sarah wasn't it?' He replaced his glasses. Looked down at the folder and flipped back through the pages. Marked the place with a stubby finger. 'Sarah Price. Died in October '96.' He paused and looked up: 'Death by misadventure.'

'I remember,' Greg said. 'Don't need you to remind me.'

'Sorry,' Bonnington said. Face a map of concern. 'Didn't mean to tread on private grief.' He flipped the pages back. 'You were a nipper at the time –'

'Seven.'

'Just seven? And you're what – fifteen, sixteen now?'

'Yeah,' Greg said. 'Fifteen.'

'You got over Sarah's death? You're fully recovered?'

'Her name was Sarah,' he said. 'Sair-er. Not Sar-ah.'

'OK,' Bonnington said. 'No need to lose your rag.' He looked down, pulled a pen from his jacket pocket and made a note in the file; placed a star against one of the paragraphs.

As he wrote, so Greg looked at the side of his head,

noted the cut of his jaw, the turn of his neck – and found himself suddenly dragged through the years so that he was staring again through a sash window at home, looking down into the street. There was a grey Ford parked on the other side of the hedge. A man with dark hair touched with grey. His mother leaning on his shoulder; her hand spread round his neck. Her fingers pulling at his hair.

Peter Bonnington.

He looked down, the breath knocked out of his seven-year-old body. At the foot of the stairs, Sarah lying dead. Now this.

'But,' said Bonnington, 'we don't want to revisit such distressing episodes –'

'It was—'

'An accident? But you weren't able to answer the police officer when you were asked to account for what happened. That's so, isn't it?' said Bonnington. 'You remained silent, if I recall correctly.'

'I was seven,' said Greg. Feeling the window pane against his fingers, the cry stilled in his mouth.

'Yes. Your mum was – elsewhere – at the time. I saw her – after the inquest. She took it very badly.'

Greg said nothing.

'You've been in trouble again –'

'What do you mean?'

'Unprovoked assault – on a student at your school – Garfield Community College, isn't it?'

'Just a fight,' he said.

' "Say that again and I'll kill you",' said Bonnington, reading from the file. 'That's a bit strong, isn't it? A bit over the top? And now,' turning the page, 'Avril King, aged eighty-two, in hospital with a suspected heart attack, after you visited her house – and stole some of her property –'

'We didn't make her ill.'

'Oh come on,' said Bonnington. 'Come on, Greg – we've got the tapes, we've got the evidence – not just from yesterday, but about your violent conduct at school – the unresolved business over your sister –'

'Leave it out,' he said. 'Sarah's death – what's that got to do with it?'

Bonnington didn't react. Just sat and watched. He turned a page in the file. He said: 'Let's move on. You met with your friend – yesterday?'

'Inderjit,' said Greg.

'Yes,' said Bonnington, finding the place on the sheet. 'Inderjit Sandhu. You've been trying to make sense of the higher than average leukaemia cases for a small part of the county?'

Greg was silent. Expressionless. Shocked. *We never mentioned leukaemia*, he thought. *We never told them*

180

what we were looking for. Just sickness, that was all. He leaned back, stared at Bonnington. That's what this is all about. They *know* about it.

'I'll take that as a "yes", shall I?' said Bonnington.

Greg shrugged. He had nothing to say.

'Right,' said Bonnington. 'A mystery.' He smiled, took off his glasses and held the arms between his fingers. 'Not just here – but throughout the country – little clusters of leukaemia or other cancers. People have been banging on for years about electricity pylons or mobile phone masts or traffic exhaust – you name it –'

A box of contaminated earth? That was the problem, wasn't it? 'We know an aircraft crashed in 1968,' Greg said. 'Leukaemia only appeared after—'

'Coincidence,' said Bonnington. 'Mere coincidence. Aircraft crashes – a train is derailed – a hospital is built and there's an emission from its incinerators – we've been there, Greg. These things have been investigated. Thoroughly.'

'So,' said Greg slowly, 'why do you want Harry King's box? If everything has been – "investigated" – like you say.'

Bonnington leaned on his elbows, looked serious. 'There are matters of national security – that I simply – simply cannot go into. You'll have to trust me on that. All we want, from you, is the box you took yesterday afternoon. In fact, we'd like to know where you've put it.'

I bet you would, thought Greg. He rubbed his eyes, breathed out heavily. 'The box – and the packet of earth – it's at home.' Watching Bonnington's face. 'I was going to show it to Mrs Brown, at school – next week. Get her opinion – see what she thought.'

'Right,' said Bonnington, stroking his chin. 'Sounds like a good idea. But we can do that for you. So – you'll give it to us. This afternoon?'

Greg looked across at him; at the carefully cut hair and steady gaze; the tailored jacket and striped shirt. The faint smell of cologne. What had his mother seen in this?

'If I don't?' Greg said. 'If I don't go with your – offer –?'

'Then you'll be booked for theft – and assault – and I could probably get the inquest on your sister reopened.' He looked across at Greg and shrugged: 'There's always new evidence.'

Thirty-four

He drove back with Dawson. Through the one-way and down past his school. There were some kids flying a stunt kite on the playing fields and he watched it loop before the car dipped down the hill to the park.

'Don't dick around,' said Dawson, at the zebra crossing.

'What –?' Greg said.

Dawson fed the wheel through his hands. 'You get the box – with the earth – and bring it straight out. I'll give you two minutes to get your arse into gear before I come in and bust you for obstructing the course of justice. Clear?'

'Sure,' said Greg, watching some old guys pitching bowls on the green. 'Whatever you say.'

They didn't speak until Dawson parked a hundred metres back from the house, on the near side. Mrs Bandaranaika sweeping her front path, turning to stare.

'If I have to switch off the ignition,' Dawson said, removing his shades. 'You're a dead man.'

'Thanks for the advice,' said Greg, unclipping the seat belt and opening the door. 'The engine won't get cold,' he added, climbing out.

The house was silent; sunlight coming through the back, catching dust motes along the corridor. The sound of a lawnmower from one of the houses in Melton Road. The swish of Mrs Bandaranaika out front.

'Hi, Sarah,' he said, looking up at the picture, the old face that stared down at him. 'Had another good day?' he asked, looking back at her closed mouth; her bright eyes. 'Business as usual then,' he said, touching the frame as he reached the top of the stairs.

He pulled the wooden box from his sock drawer and removed the package of soil. Carried the box down to the kitchen and dropped it by the stove before spreading yesterday's paper across the table. Held the half-dead poinsettia whilst he emptied the pot across the grinning face of the Prime Minister.

There were sandwich bags in the corner cupboard, and he quickly filled one with dirt.

'Ninety seconds?' he said, looking at the kitchen clock and stuffing the bag into the box. Striding down the corridor to the front door.

Dawson was listening to a jazz station by the time Greg reached the car. He handed the box through the driver's window. 'Here,' he said. 'That do you?'

The man touched the wooden surface, where the map reference was scratched. Flipped the lid and took a look.

'You better not be messing,' he said. 'Bonnington may seem the perfect gent, but—'

'You worry too much,' said Greg, patting the roof. 'See you, Mr Dawson. Take care . . .' Waving goodbye as the man replaced his sunglasses and slowly pushed the car into gear. Greg watching as the hatchback U-turned, headed into town.

He wondered how long it would take for them to work out the dirt had come from some garden centre. Sooner or later a technician would lift a phone and tell Bonnington the bad news – and then – what?

Greg phoned Middle Earth when he got back to the house, the sound of Dawson's car droning in the background, but Robin Young said: 'Raff – my mate from Leicester was over – took a sample yesterday – er – should have the analysis done – about – oh – about four.' Greg imagined him pushing his glasses up with his forefinger, his head nodding as he spoke. Lank hair touching his shoulders.

His mother got back an hour after Dawson had gone.

'Anyone ring?' she asked, coming into the lounge, where Greg was sprawled, watching an old Robert Mitchum black and white.

Yeah, he thought, the men from the Ministry. 'Nah,' he said, 'it's been really quiet. Not even a phone call.'

'What's happened to the poinsettia?' she said, 'The one by the sink?'

'Knocked it over,' he said. 'Sorry.'

'And where is it now?'

'Compost heap. Looked three-quarters dead, anyhow,' he said, watching the screen.

'Greg, that was a Christmas present – from a child at school – it just needed some water, that's all.'

'You want me to go out and resurrect it?' he said.

She didn't say anything for a second; like everything was thrown into shadow. 'I don't know about you sometimes,' she said. 'Sometimes – I – I simply don't recognise you.'

After a moment, she went back to the kitchen, and Greg could hear her turfing stuff into the cupboards; afternoon radio chattering about another crisis in the Middle East. He allowed Mitchum to fade away; thought about his dead sister; about his mother and Bonnington.

Inderjit called just after three.

'Just come out,' she said.

'Yeah?' Greg said.

'No change. Nannaji's – holding his own. The doctor said that – you know – he might stay that way for a while. But – but – you know – he won't –'

She paused to blow her nose.

'I'll come over,' Greg said.

'Yeah,' she said. 'That would be good.' The sound of a police car, getting closer. 'I'll be at the Wilton Avenue entrance, by the flowerpots.'

'OK,' he said. 'Give me ten minutes.'

His mother was indifferent when he explained the mercy call. She looked up from reading the paper, said: 'I don't know what to believe, Greg. Whether you're going to do as you say – or get yourself into more trouble.'

'This is the real thing, Mum,' he said. 'The genuine article. Giving comfort to the grief-stricken, and all that.'

'OK. You'd better be back by 4.30 at the very latest.'

Thirty-five

The Primrose Garden Hospice was just off the London Road. A rambling, red-brick house that spread the best part of a hundred metres along the street. There was a small car park on the left and on the wall, by the gate, a couple of large stone pots of flowering plants.

When he arrived, Inderjit was leaning against the wall, hands in her pockets and a frown screwing up her face.

'Thanks for coming,' she said, as he got off his bike.

'How're you doing?'

She just shrugged and looked down at the verge. She'd been crying – he could see that from the red rims around her eyes. 'It's just a matter of comforting Nanniji. They said that – that it's not likely that Nannaji will – regain consciousness. He'll – you know – carry on sleeping.'

'He's not in pain or anything?'

'No – no. He's wired up to this machine. He doesn't suffer.' A hint of a smile as she blew her nose.

'Oh,' Greg said, and leaned against the wall next to her. Listened to the bees. Wondered what else to say. 'Been over to the police station. This morning. They're all over – bugged your call yesterday – they know about the earth. Oh – and Mrs King had a heart attack last night – the police said it was because they told her we'd swiped the box –'

'Then we should return it,' Inderjit said. 'No one else should be injured because of this thing.' Her clear brown eyes staring into his face; voice steady; face set.

'They know about the leukaemia, Inderjit. We never told them. But they know. It's some kind of big secret.'

She was silent for a minute or two, as if pondering the significance of what he was saying. Then she said slowly, 'So – the air crash caused people to get sick and they've hushed everything up. Hidden it, even though – people like Nannaji –'

'We need to find out about 1968, Inderjit,' he said gently, touching her arm. 'And then decide. We don't know anything, at the moment.'

She shrugged. 'Maybe – but – it seems dangerous.'

'Yeah, about as ugly as they come –' a voice from across the street. The vowels stamped down; each word trodden into place. Fraser.

He was standing with Suzie Marlowe; hands rammed into his pockets, hair covering his forehead; smile like polythene.

'Don't let us interrupt,' he said.

'Don't they look sweet?' she said. 'Love's young dream.'

'You're funny,' Inderjit said.

'I've come into some money,' said Fraser, crossing the road, hands pulled free. Suzie Marlowe at his side, grinning.

'Yeah?' Greg said. 'Really? What you do, rob the piggy-bank?'

'Nah – not this time, killer,' he said, looking down the road. 'Seems you owe me compensation. For that "unprovoked assault" in school the other day.'

'Yeah,' said Suzie, looking serious. 'There were witnesses.'

'Where's all this come from?' Greg said. 'You're not bright enough to have worked that out.'

'Legal advice, my friend,' said Fraser.

'Oh – right,' he said, conscious of Inderjit's hand on his arm. 'Employ your own team of lawyers now?'

Fraser didn't say anything, just looked down the street, face slightly red. When he turned he said: 'You're a liability, Price – I know about you – about you and your kid sister—'

He didn't get any further; didn't get to finish the sentence, before my fist had landed in his face and he'd fallen into the road. I remember Suzie screaming, her hands pressed against her mouth and Inderjit heaving on my arm – but there was something else: the sound of an engine revving and hot tyres on tarmac.

Both Fraser and Marlowe were looking at this black saloon that was belting towards us – and I knew, at that moment, I had to get out of there.

His bike was leaning against the wall and he was in the saddle and pushing down the pavement within a couple of seconds of Fraser hitting the ground. He didn't have time to yell, 'See you,' to Inderjit, before he took the cut-through by the chippy on the corner of Wells Street. Heard the sound of the car stopping behind.

He took the track that ran up the backs of the houses running parallel with Wells – working out that the police would be keeping to the roads; checking the pavements.

The track was hidden behind a couple of refuse bins – and it was all uphill, smothered with weeds. At the top, across the road, there was an old red-brick factory – Stephenson's Shoes – that had been closed a few years. It led out to Scotton Road, opposite the filling station. The chainlink was holed in a couple of places and it was easy to push through and cross the forecourt; take the passageway down the side of the building.

He could hear sirens getting closer and he just leaned against the brickwork, listening for overclocked engines, the sound of padding feet, the cry of, 'Stay exactly where you are. Don't move!'

He watched the traffic on the main road, pulled back from the lights; saw a squad car barge past, two-tone racketing, and then pushed his bike through the nettles and found the gap in the fence.

There was no sign of law enforcement as he crossed Scotton Road and biked into the supermarket car park. Zig-zagged round people pushing their trolleys and made the exit to the slope that led down to Southfield Avenue and Middle Earth.

There wasn't anywhere else to go: no canny side streets or hidden tracks. It was the road or nothing.

He could hear the sirens over his shoulder as he took the hill – mounted the kerb and kept to the pavement on the left, using the stretch of parked cars for cover; ignored the cry of, 'Watch where you're going!' from a young woman with her kid. He didn't have time for niceties.

The sirens seemed to be getting closer when he hit Southfield, at the roundabout. Crossed over and made the far pavement; he could see Middle Earth as he rounded the bend, the road running parallel with the railway embankment.

Robin Young was with a customer – a middle-aged guy – when Greg pushed through the door – red-faced and sweating; he could hardly speak. The customer looked puzzled, but Greg just said: 'Robin –' and the other pointed to the door behind.

'I'll see what I can do – ah – Mr Francis,' Young said, and allowed the bell to ring before shooting the bolt and coming into the back room.

'Trouble?' he said, nodding towards the sound outside.

'Tell me about it,' Greg said.

Young lifted a padded envelope from the table.

'This stuff –' touching the packet '– it's – ah – radioactive, Greg. It's dangerous. To breathe. The – ah – earth – contains radioactive particles. We've wrapped it in lead sheeting.' Eyes wide behind pale frames: 'You understand that?'

Yeah, he thought, he understood that – but then there were sirens banging away and they didn't have time to chat about nuclear physics.

'Here,' Young said, chucking over a dusty bag, 'use that.'

Thirty-six

He motioned Greg towards the outside door, muttered: 'Back way,' and pushed him into a yard packed with racks of plants and sacks of compost. He opened a gate that led out on to the road.

'Don't – ah – hang around,' he said, turning an ear to the approaching din. 'I – ah – haven't seen you – or anything.'

'Thanks,' said Greg.

His bike was at the front, propped against a railing, but there was no chance of going back and collecting it. He heard the sound of brakes and doors slamming. Another siren coming down the hill from the Leisure Centre, which would pass beneath the rail bridge, right where he was standing, in a few seconds.

He ran towards the arch, and squeezed between the brickwork and the chainlink that screened the public from the embankment. Pushed through the hawthorn and nettles and started to climb towards the railway line, ears open for shouts from below. In the distance, like the soundtrack from a war movie, the beat of helicopter blades.

'Thanks,' he muttered, squinting through the leaves, trying to get a bead on the craft, amongst the drifting clouds, specks of gulls. The squad car passed on the road below and pulled up short, at the front of Middle Earth. Greg turned his back on the chaos, broke cover and scrambled up the incline towards the freight trucks parked on the nearside. The sound of copter blades filling his head and rail cars stretching left and right as far as he could see.

'Thorson' it said on each of the wagons. Blue letters on a sandy background. Each stacked high with quarried stone. A metal canopy at either end. He crouched low on the ballast, by the rails; held on to one of the buffers, and peered into the sunlight; caught sight of the dot coming in from beyond the football ground.

He found himself edging backwards, until he was right up against the coupling that linked the cars. And still he was exposed. Probably have infrared or some such, he thought, looking up. Probably got him marked from a couple of miles away. Just a matter of calling in the filth from below.

He acted without thinking; felt the need to get away,

to get out of sight from the prowling eye, the searchlight glare of the sun. He ducked down, below the chain and coupling, between the wheels and under the freight car. Crouched down and listened to the threshing above; imagined the copter hovering at a few hundred feet, turning in the air as two pairs of eyes scanned the ground, muttered instructions.

It was cool in this shadowy world and the air stank of oil and dust. He looked through the wheels at the fringe of grass and the tops of bushes. Listened to the shouts of the coppers; felt the air tremble.

And then he heard the wagon jerk; felt the coupling tense; the rattle from the diesel ahead. And still the air was chopped and diced.

Get out now, he thought, and it's all over. Everything just chucked away, wasted. Worse: they'd do him for theft, assault – even reopen the inquest on Sarah and charge him with killing her. Like Bonnington said.

He imagined the disappointed look on his mother's face, when she came into the police station – meeting in some interview room; his father behind, all dark suit and grey eyes.

He reached up and touched the cold metal; felt the weight and strength.

No way back, he thought, and crouched lower; watched for the turn of wheels; calculated how low he'd have to get without having his head torn off, as the train hauled out of the station.

And then, there was a slight change in the atmosphere; as though a switch had been pressed, a light turned out. The helicopter was moving towards the Leisure Centre and the A14. He could see it, tilted nose down, hovering over the tennis courts by the lake. Scouring the bushes and pathways between the estate and the dual carriageway.

They'd given up on the railway line and the embankment. Worked out that he'd slipped away, had crossed the road and made for cover down by the water.

The train gave another lurch and there was a shout from the station. He edged towards the gap between the sets of wheels; looked at the polished rims and worn tracks – and crawled through, even as there was a final blast of the throttle – and the wheels started to turn.

I wasn't going to hang around. There was no chance I was going to let Bonnington grab hold of the softpack stuffed in the bag at my feet.

I just lifted a foot, raised an arm – and climbed the steps leading on to one of the freight cars. Swung under the overhang and crouched on the narrow platform, with my back against the cold metal. There was a squad car below, the gantry all reds and blues – and that was it. Goodbye and good riddance.

As we steamed out of Gretford, I pulled out my mobile and tossed it overboard. I didn't want some satellite to use it as a homing device or whatever they had. The police could send out a full search party, for all I cared, and spend a few hours turning over the rusted cans and smashed glass at the foot of the embankment. But I wouldn't be there.

Thirty-seven

As he watched the passing of trees and fields, listened to the racket of the freight trucks, so he thought about the parcel that Robin Young had thrust into his hands. Heard again the anxious, 'This stuff – it's radioactive.'

He watched as the train bumped and rumbled alongside the canal and swung north into Leicestershire, the sun touching his left cheek. Wondered about his mother and what she would think when he didn't show; when the police hammered at the front door.

But there was too much to worry about and he just shunted the family stuff to one side: looked at the scenery and thought about 1968. He didn't know what had been going on back then, at the end of the sixties, but when that aircraft flipped into the ground, it sorted the future for several hundred, maybe several thousand people – firefighters who attended the blaze; people who lived downwind of the crash – kids wandering to school that next day; people going to work, walking to the shops – anyone doing anything.

And as the wagons creaked and jerked through that afternoon it became obvious that the plane hadn't just left a hole in a field.

It had been carrying a bomb. A nuclear device. Explained why the police were turning somersaults. The plane got into trouble, the crew had ejected – and then the aircraft had exploded in the countryside, just over from Creighton Wood. The bomb casing must have been damaged by the impact – and radioactive stuff got spewed into the night.

It made every kind of sense. Changed everything – his own life, Nannaji's – Harry King's. Some kind of chain reaction.

In the storm, with a great gale blowing, the fragments would have gone miles. Months – years later and people woke up with cancer. That's why the police were so interested in what he and Inderjit had found.

He leapt down when the train got stalled, just outside Leicester. He guessed there were lights or something up ahead and couldn't see any future in hanging around.

He scrambled up the bank and climbed over a fence; walked through a few acres of playing field before he hit the main road. It was twenty to five by the clock hanging outside the chemist's and a road sign told him the city centre was two miles away.

He wasn't equipped for 'going on the run', because although it was a warm afternoon with just a touch of breeze, all he had were the summer clothes he stood up in; a wallet with five pounds, some odd change – and a building society debit card.

He knew that he needed to stay clear of major shopping centres, railway stations, car parks – anywhere that might have CCTV. Later, Raff would tell him to empty the building society account, outside the city. 'Wear this hat,' he said, tossing over a peaked cap. 'Low down, cover your eyes, man. They'll check the video tape when you're done.'

But that was later. That afternoon he was wondering how to survive the night. Which is where he lucked in, when he pulled from his back pocket the piece of bent card Robin Young had given him on receipt of the soil sample. The one that said Middle Earth in that swirling script. The one that had the three phone numbers for their shops in Gretford, Peterborough and – Leicester.

He knew there was nowhere to go when he ducked into the next phone box. Tapped in the numbers and eyed the pair of coppers talking to a shopkeeper ten metres to his left.

* ★ ★

He listened to the ring tone for the best part of thirty seconds before the receiver was lifted; heard the routine shop sounds and then a deep voice said: 'Hello, Middle Earth.'

'Hi,' he said breezily. 'Hi – just wanted to know if – ah – Raff was there –'

'Speaking.'

'Right –' He watched the police stroll past. 'You looked at some earth – from Gretford – yesterday?'

In the background, a shop assistant totalled someone's purchases; he could hear Raff's breathing; and the voice, when it returned, was careful, suspicious.

'What do you want to know?'

'I need to talk to you. I'm in Leicester. Need to pick your brain.'

Again, there was a pause. 'Who are you?' he said.

'Greg Price – I gave Robin Young the soil—'

'OK,' Raff said. 'I finish here in a bit. Where are you now?'

'Wigston? Somewhere like that?' He looked across the road at a sign. 'It says Welford Road—'

'Take the next bus – any bus – heading into town. Ask for the college and get off when you see a large red-brick building. Wait there.' And Raff put the phone down.

'Ninety p,' the driver said, when he climbed aboard the 15 that appeared ten minutes later. 'Give you a shout when we reach the stop.'

'Thanks,' Greg said; took a seat half way down; stared out at the string of semi-detached houses that lined the road; thought of Gretford and everything he'd left behind. Imagined telling a three-year-old Sarah what he'd been up to, how he'd escaped. Tried to imagine her, aged eleven, as they jolted into town. Probably have hated me, he thought. Some bratty kid.

He was interrupted by the driver, who'd pulled up at a set of lights: 'The college is over there,' she said, pointing at a five-storey block.

'Thanks,' Greg said, and got up to wait behind a woman with a snivelling kid clinging to her hand. Scanned ahead, but there was no one waiting at the stop.

He hung around by a newsagent's for the best part of twenty minutes before a tall black guy with dreads and crooked teeth appeared. He looked at Greg a couple of times. Said: 'You the guy with the dirt?'

'Yeah,' Greg said.

'I'm Raff,' the guy said and stuck out his hand. 'You're Greg – right?' and when Greg nodded, said: 'We'll get a drink – over at the college. Place we can talk.'

Thirty-eight

'Place we can talk,' he thought, leaning forward on the park bench that overlooked the canal. All of three weeks ago. Three weeks of ducking into the college and logging in on Raff's old user name. Waiting for the moment when he'd look up and see some guy in a black jacket and dark scowl fill the doorway.

But no one arrived and he got used to the routine of taking side streets to the college. Watching for people sitting in parked cars. Looking in the plate glass of shop windows. Back-tracking every now and then.

And he'd seen nothing: no spooks waiting to leap out and half-nelson him into a waiting car. No one hanging around street corners when he left Raff's flat. Nothing – until that last morning.

For three weeks he'd tapped out his story, trying to work out what he'd do when it was all over; where he could go; who he could speak to. And that morning, he'd slipped out of the flat in Dover Street and headed for college, in the usual way. It had been Raff's day off and Greg had left him fixing breakfast: the kitchen filled with Latin brass and bacon.

Greg hadn't reached London Road, when he remembered that he needed a spare disk and turned back.

He heard the commotion before he reached the corner. The sound of an argument – someone shouting abuse. And when he looked down the length of the road, he saw Raff, handcuffed behind his back, being held by a white guy in a red top, while a second held open the door of an unmarked car.

Greg pulled back from the corner; checked the road each way and crossed to the graveyard at the front of the Catholic church. Took shelter in the shade of the trees that lined the side-wall. Hung around for half an hour, waiting for the air to be filled with sirens; the roads jammed with screeching cars. He wondered about Raff: where he was, who he was talking to. And he wondered how they had been found out.

No point in heading for the college, he thought. There'd be police sitting at each of the consoles, waiting for him. No point in avoiding the centre of town now.

When the rain eased, he picked up his bag and sloped

off, through the roads by the train station, and took the direct route. Stopped at the Post Office to send a letter and then walked to the canal. Wandered down to the bench beyond the iron bridge.

For some time, he watched an old guy feed the swans; listened to him as he talked to the birds, coaxing them to pull bread from his hands. When the man left, trudging along the towpath, Greg pulled his notebook from his bag, propped it on his knee and after a few seconds, wrote:

Dear Sarah
You've been talking to me these few years, and I never thought to answer back, tell you how I felt.
I expect that if you were sitting here, you'd pull my arm and tell me that it's time to go home, and I think you'd be right. Time to go back and give my side of the story: say what really happened. Let the others sort out their part.
Do you remember when we used to go to the park and float paper boats on the pond? When it gets dark, I often think of our time together and how you used to throw twigs into the water, trying to sink our fleet. You made me laugh then, and sometimes I think I've never laughed since.
It's getting late, Sarah. A lot of stuff has gone under the bridge, but I'll never forget the time we had.
When I've finished here, I'm going to look east and go back

the way I came. I'm sorry I wasn't able to take better care of you.

With love – from your brother.

Greg.

He ripped the sheet from the book and made the familiar folds, turning his message inside, and shaping the long section of hull. And when he was ready, he left the towpath, crossed the strip of grass and hunkered down by the water's edge, gently pushing the boat on to the rippled surface. Watched the breeze take it out into the centre; imagined his sister looking for a stick to chuck after it.

As it slowly rocked back and forth, so he heard a voice calling from above. For a moment, he didn't pay any attention, just looked at the way the light played on the water, heard the soft lapping of the eddies touching the stone embankment.

'Greg!'

Louder this time, closer, and when he turned to his right, turned his face into the sun, it was to see a tall guy in a tracksuit jogging down the slope from the road. Behind, through the railings, the lights of the police car.

'Greg,' the guy shouted, 'hang on,' arm waving, feet pounding.

Greg stood up, looked to his left, down the stretch of canal towards the bridge at the Newarke crossing. A young kid on a bike ahead; someone walking a dog. And the sound of feet beating towards him.

'Wait!' the guy shouted and Greg took off, dropping his bag and pushing away on the balls of his feet; trying to put together the map that he'd studied in the half-light of Raff's kitchen. 'Wait!' the guy called again.

Greg made the bridge and ran on as the canal swung to the left and right, past the faded brickwork of the paint factory; past the new car showroom. When he checked, he saw that the guy behind had dropped back, was talking into a radio, and presently, as the canal ran parallel to the river and the footpath became a bridge over a weir, he heard the call of a siren. Pushing through traffic ahead.

He stopped then. Held on to the bridge railings and dropped his head. Allowed his breathing to return to normal; for his heart to stop thumping. Heard the fall of water tumbling below. Felt the sweat sliding down his chest. Knew that he hadn't shaken off his pursuer.

'We need to talk.'

The guy again, a hundred metres away, less. Trotting towards him. Arms in the air, smile plastered to his face.

Greg turned to his right and saw a couple of uniformed coppers running along the path beside the fretted wall of an old warehouse. Black body armour against white shirts; truncheons banging against their sides.

Ahead, the sweep of the river, dotted with moorhens and mallards. A swan below digging at the feathers beneath its wing. And the pursuer getting so close that Greg could hear his breath, hear the crush of gravel beneath his feet. Only one way to go.

Detective Sergeant Morgan was less than fifty metres away now; saw Greg look back at him. Like he was smiling or something. And then, Greg raised his left hand, like it was in some kind of salute and the next moment – he'd swung his right leg on to the rail, levered himself up – and dropped over the side.

'Vanished in a blur,' Morgan said later. 'Gone in a second.'

Greg hit the base of the weir with a shock that knocked all the breath from his body and he found himself pitched forward as his feet failed to hold on to the greasy slope. He fell so that his head smashed against the timber of an old mooring post and in the sudden pain, saw the day turn into night.

Thirty-nine

'Letter for you, Inderjit,' said Mr Everett, passing over the blue envelope.

'Probably from her boyfriend,' said Sheetal. 'Sending her a love letter.'

'Thanks,' Inderjit said and tucked it into her bag.

'Aren't you going to open it?' said Davindar. 'Find out what it says?'

'Later,' she said and looked out of the window, towards the church and the green fields beyond. The hills above Northampton were hazed over and she knew it would be raining by lunchtime; thunder cracking in from the west.

Two minutes before, Suliman had trudged into the form room, dragging his bag and muttering some excuse. Didn't catch her eye when he turned to sit down. Like he blamed her for Greg's vanishing trick.

As she looked outside, she was suddenly back by the war memorial, scrunched up on the bench and watching the tall lad in black jeans cycle over from the village shop. He looked up and suddenly saw her, a smile breaking his face. Almost in spite of himself, she thought. Dismounting and coming round to where she sat. Excited by the news he brought; excited by this chance to get to see her. Except that he didn't know that then.

'Right,' said Everett, 'Mr Jordan has asked me to collect any late maths projects.' He looked over his glasses. 'So, let's be having them.'

She remembered the ragged look as Greg had leapt on to his bike that last afternoon; the air filled with the car accelerating down the street. And then? – After the police interview – waiting for a text, a signal that he was all right, somewhere safe.

That was two weeks ago, three. Now this – a letter in Greg's scratchy hand. Leicester postmark. 25th June smudging the stamp. Last Friday.

'Right,' said Mr Everett, standing up and looking down at a scrap of paper. 'This week's news. First up, there's going to be a change in the lunchtime arrangements, because of the building work in the canteen . . .'

She remembered the knock on the door, three days

after Nannaji's death. A couple of taps and the shadow through the net curtain. Inderjit had known who it was, the moment she pulled back the door and looked down. A woman with faded blonde hair and a face unsettled by worry.

'Inderjit?' the woman said. 'Are you Inderjit Sandhu?'

'Come in,' Inderjit said, and led the way into the lounge. She sat opposite Greg's mother and listened to her questions. Heard her talk about Sarah, the dead three-year-old; about the sleepwalking son.

'He – witnessed Sarah's death,' she said. 'He had some counselling – but – he never really got over it. None of us did. Sent himself messages from her. But –' She stopped, made a hopeless gesture with her hand. 'He's – never been in any – you know – real trouble – Not until these last weeks.' She attempted a smile. 'If you knew where he was, you'd tell me. Wouldn't you?'

'Yes,' Inderjit said. 'But – he hasn't phoned. Or anything.'

'I'll leave my number,' the woman said. 'Just in case,' and she reached into her bag, her hand trembling.

The bell signalled the end of registration and Inderjit left the others and went out to the playground by the library. Sat where she'd been with Greg that day, when Fraser had come over and they'd had the fight.

She pulled the exercise paper from the envelope Everett had given her; noted the blue ballpoint, the haphazard handwriting:

Dear Inderjit

It seems ages since we met and I've just about run out of time. We'll see each other again. I'm sure of that – maybe go to the ten-pin and beat Suli and Dilshad.

I know that you've had too much to cope with, and I know you cared for your grandfather and tried to do your best for him. People can't do any more, I think.

I liked working with you – you know that. You taught me a lot – maybe to grow up a bit – although 'three counties' was below the belt. Thought about it the other day, when I was by the canal. There's an old iron bridge down there – girders bent over and stitched with a cross piece. A whole packet of fun.

You might want to check it out sometime, tell me what you think. But there's no hurry.

The canal swarms with ducks and swans at the moment – you'd really like it.

I have to go now, before it gets too late: say goodbye to someone from the past.

I really do like you, by the way.

Greg x

She touched the letters; felt the pressure on the paper. Noticed where he'd run some of the words together, as if he'd been in a hurry. And as she read, so she knew that Greg was signalling danger. The package was safe, hidden – she picked out the signpost pointing to the canal bridge, but there was something else. Felt, not stated – and as the cars and lorries swept past on the main road, she knew she would never see his careless smile or hear his casual laugh again.

Across the playground, the firedoor opened and Mrs Yardley walked into the sunlight. She had a register in her hand and she paused when she saw Inderjit; her mouth set in a firm line.

She came over and sat down – and was silent. As though she was waiting for some signal, so that she could start talking. Later, Inderjit realised that Mrs Yardley had sat there, trying to find the right words; trying to figure out the right tone, to blunt the blow, make it all less terrible than it was.

When she spoke, she touched Inderjit's arm and said quietly: 'I have some really sad news to tell you.'

Inderjit said nothing. Ahead, the scatter of crisp packets and sweet wrappers. Behind, a blackbird in the undergrowth.

She looked at Mrs Yardley and said: 'It's about Greg, isn't it?' feeling his words beneath her fingertips. Not wanting to hear all this from someone else. 'You don't have to tell me – I know – he's not coming back. Is he?'

Mrs Yardley looked down. 'There's been – an accident,' she said quietly. 'I don't know all the details, but – he isn't coming back.'

Inderjit stood up then, needing to leave this woman, with her neat suit and calm voice. Her talk of an 'accident'. She took a deep breath and wiped her eyes. She shook her head when Mrs Yardley reached for her arm.

'It's not over,' Inderjit said and lifted her school bag.

She turned away then, walked back across the playground to the firedoors. She felt the breeze in her face, like a memory; felt the words in her hand.

Mrs Yardley watched the girl pause to pull the handle, and then she was gone, leaving only the movement of the door, sunlight flashing on glass.

DEAD NEGATIVE

Nick Manns

'They stare through the bars; each framed by the cross-patterning of the metal; each its own portrait. Behind, there's the square of a window; the light breaking up the bars like heat. And as you look at the picture, you see all the grids and squares of the composition: how the four guys are boxed and packaged and contained.

Elliot's father was a war photographer, renowned for 'shooting the truth'. He died in strange circumstances in Paris. The mystery has never been solved.

Jaspreet is Elliot's friend, target of the school bullies. He relies on Elliot's unstinting, loyal friendship.

Now these two troubled threads of Elliot's life are drawing inexorably together.

SEED TIME

Nick Manns

To begin with he couldn't make anything out in the shadows thrown by the trees, but then his eyes following Michael's arm, he saw a black shape take form in the grey . . .

It was Michael's idea – excluded from school and reckless since the death of his father. 'Time to pick up the past,' he said.

They cycled to the heath on a Friday. Tony played truant, lying to his parents – trying not to think of their faces already stretched taut by threatening financial disaster.

Michael drew it from the water – a long-buried treasure dripping slime and algae. With it came new conflict – and new hope . . .

From the author of *Control-Shift*, shortlisted for the North East Book Award and the Branford Boase Award.

'Nick Manns is on a winner here!' *School Librarian*

CONTROL-SHIFT

Nick Manns

'The house is calm. Maybe because night doesn't press against the windows and the events of last winter are finally over; because somewhere a young man who felt he'd failed in his own life has seen the demons driven away in ours and no longer walks the dark . . .'

In their new home in an old country house, Graham's father designs a computer-guided, state-of-the-art weapons system.

But Graham and his sister Matty sense they are not alone in the house. Bleak and terrifying secrets hover – secrets that will shift the very foundations of their lives . . .

Shortlisted for the North East Book Award and the Branford Boase Award.

'a talent for the ghostly real as the past permeates the present.' *Books for Keeps*

'An uncompromising novel that will leave readers wide-eyed and breathless.' *Amazon.co.uk*